ADVENTURE
OF HEROES

ADVENTURE OF HEROES

RESOLUTION
VOLUME III

SEAN L JOHNSON

iUniverse

ADVENTURE OF HEROES
RESOLUTION VOLUME III

iUniverse books may be ordered through booksellers or by contacting:

iUniverse
1663 Liberty Drive
Bloomington, IN 47403
www.iuniverse.com
1-800-Authors (1-800-288-4677)

ISBN: 978-1-5320-9033-2 (sc)
ISBN: 978-1-5320-9047-9 (e)

Library of Congress Control Number: 2019920131

Print information available on the last page.

iUniverse rev. date: 12/18/2019

Planet Xeiar, Orbiting Celestial star Junio's Moon in the Namorant Dimension

Many, many, many years ago... There was a dispute raging among the ten planets orbiting Celestial Star Sol, the Namorant Dimension's principal star. The ten planets were members of different alliances. The Xeiar Greats, full of pride in their victory over nature, decided to move the planet off on its own, far away from Sol.

A few planets were at war with each other and didn't see their races being completely wiped out, becoming extinct.

There's a belief in Namorant and Isolated Dimensions... That those who lose their way, becoming corrupt and merciless, despite the circumstances, are condemned and banned to a gloomy dark place, where life is as short as cruel. It's not Darkiel, but a darker prison dimension.

If one good thing had to come out of those confusing times, was the fact that the Xeiar civilization, and its allies, were forced to enter a new age of evolution, and, most important, elevation. An era in which magic is revealed as being technology and knowledge in its most advanced stage.

The strongest wizards of planet Xeiar... They are the stronghold, the ones who have the responsibility of dealing with the toughest problems in times of serious crisis. And of course, erasing them. King Makliton's ancestors' granted special permissions on Great Xeiar Wizards, past and future, to use whatever methods necessary to maintain peace.

These selected wizards, by a series of many difficult trials, are selected in a group of three. Sometimes they're chosen one by one after one dies for any reason.

Magis is the Majestic leader over the Earth element, Amras has the equivalent position, but over the Air element, and finally, Kyiah: the only female of this tri-force, rules over the Sea element. These are their primary advantages and their skill-sets.

These special wizards have their meeting place, an exclusive assembly hall with a half crescent moon-shaped table and three royally crafted chairs rooted to the floor behind.

Above, on the polished ornamental ceiling, to what appear to be almond-colored silk drapes in the shape of a wreath and the center of it written beautifully, Grand Xesus. The room feels warm and inviting, where they hold their reunions, meetings, and acts as their base of operations.

This entire place, named Grand Xesus, is a tower, with four floors. Outside is a hue of blue and grey's, and decorated with small statues of the main deities of Xeiar, the past Great Wizards. They're forming a perimeter in front of the tower.

Beyond Xesus lies an enormous and mysterious forest with respective mountains. The forest has a decent amount of creatures, each possessing a different special ability and/or livable asset to its being. These species keep their... changes. Some of them turned out somewhat powerful and have enhanced mutant aberrations. They're very intelligent as well, and for this reason, it was never a hypothesis to hunt them down because their hiding techniques are remarkable. Some deep areas of the woods are, so to speak, forbidden because if some Xeiarians dare to explore them, they may never be seen again or at least seen alive again.

We find Magis, Amras, and Kyiah gathered in the main room of Grand Xesus, sitting down. They are speaking about an important matter. Two rouge wizards, who have been locked and isolated in Valdesmon, a parallel dimensional prison, managed to escape and there are matters to this event.

MAGIS. Yes. This situation is of relative importance.

AMRAS. What do we know, for now, regarding their intentions?

MAGIS. So far, it appears they want to take over planet Earth. To conquer, control, and possibly turn the planet's inhabitants into their slaves.

KYIAH. Earth?! In that "Isolated" Dimension... *In disbelief.* Does that planet still exists?

MAGIS. Heh. That surprised me too.

KYIAH. Earthlings lead themselves to extinction. After wars, and consuming all resources, they turn their planet into a cosmic trash can.

MAGIS. They did turn their planet into a "cosmic trash can", Kyiah. But life is stubborn when it comes up to its possible extinction. Humans will always be like viruses, in many ways. They are hard to kill, they destroy everything, and when we think they are gone for good... they just reveal themselves, here and there, in new growing communities. *Adjusting the purple robe, hanging over the right side of his shoulder.*

KYIAH. 'Specially when you belong to a species that practices cannibalism. A dead brother quickly becomes your next meal.

AMRAS. Think you're over exaggerating, Kyiah.

MAGIS. Well, if it is or not. What I'm saying is quite unusual. I don't nurture any particular affection towards Earth's humanity...

AMRAS. Tell us something we don't know.

MAGIS. *Pauses, eyeing Amras suspiciously for seconds then continues speaking.* ...the fact is, it was once an important civilization in their galaxy, The Milky Way. It had its highlights! Hm. *Thinks for a minute.*

KYIAH. I'm confused rather you love the human race or wish they die on their own accord.

MAGIS. *He laughs.* Heh. I think we should help them. Us... The three Xeiar Gods alone.

KYIAH. We will not benefit being anywhere near or around those rouge mages! *Speaking passionately strong.* What?! Do we become emperors of another planet? *Exhales.* They could become too ambitious... *Turns and her eyes look at Amras.*

AMRAS. *Eyes swaying side to side, looking at his fellow wizards.* What?

KYIAH. Pfft. *Shakes her head.* I know how you feel about Earth and assume we were once the same race just moved to another world a very long, long, long time ago.

AMRAS. *Stutters, as he always did in the past speaking to Kyiah.* I –

MAGIS. *Laughs.* Hahahaa. We got sidetracked. Let's get back on topic.

KYIAH. So, who are these wizards?

MAGIS. Two allies... *Pauses for a second.* ...that had been cast out on individual but respective orders, and hence, lost their privileges within the dimension to which they once lived. It seems, decades after what happened with the two, they rebelled against Xeiar Law to become outlaws. Decades ago, the two caused a lot of damage. The former Xeiar Great, Boigos, had them captured and brought before him to stand trial. But, of course, they couldn't be kept in any normal jail, for common barriers and walls would not hold adolescence. And so they were sent to another dimension, Valdesmon. The outcast wizards, however, revealed themselves too wise and too strong.

KYIAH. So how do you think the two managed to escape when their magical abilities were stripped?

MAGIS. I do not remember, and I don't know. Maybe Boigos was too sloppy and didn't remove their powers.

AMRAS. They were able to break the barrier, by opening a portal which allowed them to get into another dimension.

KYIAH. Although they were not strong enough to overthrow the forces of Law, still, before they left their prison. They didn't produce a massacre or slaughter... yet. Wonder what they're planning?

MAGIS. There's a sinister feel out there. This we know. You two can feel this strange vibe, am I right?

AMRAS. The feeling of death returning? Yeah, I have been feeling it for months now.

KYIAH. They'll be defeated before any death occurs.

Unlike Magis and Kyiah, Amras didn't feel too inclined preparing a mission to liberate the distant planet Earth.

MAGIS. *Looking at Amras's expression, half concerned.* I do understand and respect your point of view. *Reading the youngest's Greats mind.* So, in your opinion, we should organize a defense squad for Earth's survival?

AMRAS. *Shakes away his thoughts, realizing the two staring at him questionably.* No!! Not at all, Magis.

MAGIS. Your concerns regarding these inferior beings becoming dangerous rulers one day in the Milky Way are highly questionable. I do not agree, but these kinds of thoughts present realistic outcomes. Our magic creates situations based on our emotions... You should know.

AMRAS. My apologies, Magis. Forgive my selfish mind for producing such thoughts. I just have concerns about a race which resemble our own, but lack in certain skill-sets.

KYIAH. I wouldn't go that far, but I can hardly imagine a couple of Earthlings when they learn how to use magic, will be able to build something out of Earth much less using it to become more powerful. Disregard Earth is how I feel. They have their heroes and we should leave our planet, and our tasks, on Xeiar. This is not of our concern. Let us not play heroes. We are not the Universal League of Justice...

AMRAS. They are of our kind, Kyiah.

KYIAH. I stand by what I said.

AMRAS. All right, so to you, there's no importance in saving Earth?

MAGIS. It's a matter of priorities, but I have to agree with her. Our planet, our galaxy should be ours. Plus,

Amras, there is something else you need to know. I wasn't going to say anything, but since you are the only one who believes the three of us should fly to Earth and deal with the invading wizards... I have no alternative.

Amras looked at Magis, very intrigued and Magis looked back at him. They're all making eye contact right now.

MAGIS. One of the rebellious wizards is your little brother, Amras. You still remember, right?

This did come as a shock to Amras because he so tried to forget the reckless actions that his little brother put him through as he was training and learning how to become a Great Wizard.

After losing both blood relatives during his teenage years (Xeiarians age different), he needed to take care of his little brother. He had no clue how to combat the behavior.

He had a particularly love-hate relationship with his brother. The two were close, but after their parents died Amras didn't understand why his little brother was always the rebellious one. He kept his brother out of serious trouble up until a specific event; one he could not control so the Greats had to step in.

Amras spaces out for a full minute. He has to answer quickly, without losing his calm, and his self-control. But at the same time, he needed to think. And so, in a few seconds, he found a solution.

AMRAS. I appreciate the sensible information, Magis. The keyword here, is, in fact, sensible. And so, both you and Kyiah will understand this; I need to think alone. *Stands up, pushing his chair under the table.* Maybe an hour or two, no more than that. And I will do it in the forests. The forbidden forests, around the hideous creatures. It will be the best way to reflect, and at the same time, be prepared to fight, and remind me what war does.

MAGIS. *Laughs.* Ah-ha! Of course, my friend. I understand your decision. I might join you later because I too have grown restless sitting around and not engaging in a scuffle in a very long time. As the eldest member... You go. *Waves him off.* You go and be careful. But, we will be waiting for your decision.

Kyiah didn't speak any words, but she did gesture to Amras as he left the tower.

The Great Air Wizard left the tower, and he started walking to the forest.

To the "forbidden woods". Not all parts of the forests were dangerous. At least, in general. Of course, anything could happen.

About fifteen Earth minutes later...

Amras penetrated the woods, fusing his thoughts with his awareness, regarding his surroundings.

The trees were so tall, and he thought that the forest was relatively dark because the sun wouldn't pass through them.

In the first minutes, everything was quiet. But soon enough, he started to listen to something. Discrete noises. Movements. Finally, the first creature was there. Most likely watching him.

The wizard, using his power of controlling the Air, produced a strong wind, and the bushes in which the creature was hiding, moved away, and the being was revealed.

It was a Grizzle, a furry short little thing, with small red eyes, and a stretching mouth, with sharp teeth, revealing blood. It must've just had its daily snack.

As the Grizzle was revealed, he attacked Amras. The Wizard thought about using his staff. He was good with it and could have easily slaughtered the poor creature. But he just used another wind spell, a moderately stronger one than before. He produced a micro-typhoon, which captured the creature and took him – fast and furiously – far away, deep into the woods.

AMRAS. It's not these creatures fault they are like this. In the last resort, of course, we must kill them. As they want to kill us and consume us. But only in the last resort. Our wars... all wars... they are not the common's fault. It's the leaders' fault. They decide to spread chaos and destruction, in order to pursue their ambitions. And all life, all spirits, suffer. *His eyes raise to the clouds in the sky above.* I am sorry, brother. But it is not the Earth's common man, or common beast, that you wish to become a tyrant. As it was not the Earth's common man, or common beast, that, in the past, their leaders sent you away to meet your demise. My decision stands. I must go, and protect Earth. Regardless what ramifications I cause along the way... *Exhales.* I'll fix my mistake.

These were Amras's thoughts, as he left the forest, and again, walked back towards Grand Xesus. He would try, the best as he could, to convince both Magis and Kyiah that they should arrange a saving mission, on behalf of Earth. If he, Amras, was willing to fight his brother for such cause, how could they not?

The answer became no. Since there was no killing from these two escaped wizards who fled to Earth, the Greats did not see a need to leave Xeiar. There was no real threat. Amras sighed and went outside to watch flying mammals frolic cheerfully outside Xesus by the flower garden meadows.

SATURDAY, MARCH 4TH 2107, 10:00 P.M. *(EARTH TIME)*
Valdesmon Prison Dimension

No way to tell the time in this place. It's dark with no light. The two wizards, who have lived here since they were young pre-teens after their crimes, learned slowly how to find one another. In the beginning, they were scared and couldn't see anything. But, with time they learned how to see in other ways without using their eyes; their cries were heard and Asari managed to listen out for others. He eventually found Malee.

Those who don't emit any noise does so in a different way.

Presently, Asarios is alone in the dark. Maleena as well. They're in their own created "rooms" (or spaces) which they each fabricated by thought. This prison works upon what a person's thoughts create. Depending on the situation, whatever you think becomes reality. Too bad one can't think up escape.

The two wizards are individually pondering their first day in this terrible place.

FLASHBACK...

The atmosphere around the village was unusually quiet for a busy afternoon. There was no sight of children who normally would be playing around within the fence. Older wizards would be returning to their homes after a long day of collecting herbs and concoctions for their spells. This day, however, things were far from normal; something was out of place.

There was no denying the tense and strange atmosphere inside the courtroom that evening. The small stage was filled, with other people struggling in tiptoes to get a glimpse of whatever was happening through the crowd of Xeiarians. On the stage area, the three wizards of Xeiar were sitting in their usual positions just behind the wizard guards wearing their usual long cloaks and huge hats that shed shadows so dark that their faces remained invisible. The three are the most respected wizards in the Xeiar Kingdom; even the king dared not do anything against their counsel.

Today was a unique day. The witnesses, to remain confidential, in the crowd, were desperate to see if this power balance between the judiciary and the executive power of the great wizardly kingdom would withstand today's case; for it was not just any other case.

Sitting in the front row of the busy stage was the eldest and wisest Great Wizard Boigos to date, who was dressed in the ceremonious attire that made him look like a heavenly being even to the eyes of these great wizards. The usually uptight Great looked more or less like he already decided on a strict punishment. Boigos isn't your usual grandfather type, he's typically rude and strictly by the ancient books aka rules. A man with a long Van Dyke Beard, bushy and no mustache. He has a fair share of wrinkles, leading he might be well over two million years old, but in the equivalent to humans from Earth… eighty years old.

Just a few meters from the fence separating the village from the "Forbidden Lands" a crowd stood in a circle whispering and murmuring in low tones. At the center of the circle, that was getting larger with every passing minute, was a young boy around eleven years of age. He looked frightened and shaken as he stared at the guards who stood in front of the stage where the Great Wizards dealt with the wronged, i.e. "bad people". They're keeping eye contact on the two youngsters, looking down on them.

UNNAMED WIZARD GUARD. Have you heard about the Forbidden Lands? *Asking in a voice that made the little boy shudder.*

ASARI. Y – Yes, I – I – I have. *He answered nervously.*

UNNAMED WIZARD GUARD. And you know the punishment for trespassing?

The boy was too scared to answer now. He looked at his elder brother, who showed no signs of grief at all in his attractive, well-proportioned, and imposing healthily strength attributes. He stood like a soldier, quiet and obedient. He stood at the front row of the crowd as if expecting him to pitch in for him. Even as his brother trembled, throwing quick, scared glances at the jury as they whispered amongst themselves, the older boy just kept his calm; not even once did he raise his hand to comfort the little boy. He watched together with the other villagers. A teardrop fell from the little boy's eyes before he turned his head, looking away from his brother.

Malee, the charming and scholarly daughter of King Makliton, had found herself in the worst situation an eleven-year-old could probably find herself in. Malee, a rather small princess than average, but her round face, long strands of perfect silky hair, and glistening pink eyes all in awe. There was hate as the indifferent stares from the jury and the accusing glances from the crowd. What she feared the most was the helpless look from her parents. She stood right beside the young boy. She didn't make a sound nor did she make eye contact with anyone.

Suddenly, the court was silent as one of the jury members stood up.

GREAT WIZARD MAGIS. Ladies and gentlemen, the jury has their final verdict.

The voice seemed to echo from afar in Malee's head. She was trying to replay the events that had gotten her to this situation, trying to find out where they had gone wrong. The past weeks she never saw Asari before, but eventually, she did.

GREAT WIZARD ANIELIAS. *Her long gorgeous locks of olive hair swaying as the wind moves gracefully through each strand.* What the children did is wrong... *She continued.* We, being the Great Wizards of Xeiar, will punish them accordingly. *She sat down slowly in the seat as murmurs were going that suddenly went silent.*

Moments later, as the three wizards rose to their feet, it was difficult to tell which one of them was speaking.

GREAT WIZARD BOIGOS. We find the two of you guilty for causing the destruction of millions on planet Xirxion and for the release of dangerous creatures to planet Vexion which cannot be undone. You two – *He pauses for a second.* – Led magical Xeiar creatures to planet Vexion and under our laws, you will be banished immediately!

Malee gasped. Asari let out a desperate sob, looking at his brother who just stared emotionless as the two guards approached them from behind. The King walked closer and begged. He pleaded and this was strange because as King he was over the Greats. Unfortunately, not in this case.

Malee wasn't there. She had her head down looking at the stage floor. Her powers strangely started reacting to her mood. Makliton saw this and decided to go to her side. Her father had seen her mood changing and the moment he tried to touch her hand, to ease her powers, he was cursed to an unknown place. Perhaps obliterated. No one knew how to undo the spell her powers had done. Everyone saw this and believed it was intentional.

The young princess's powers reacted and the king was gone in the blink of an eye. One would guess he had just been transported to another place, but spectators and the Greats thought this was intentional and cursed at her. For an eleven-year-old, she had only done it in self-defense and it took her a while to realize just how consequential her actions were. When she did, she dropped to her knees and wept.

With an added sentence, young Malee was accused of letting her emotions get the best of her. She heard what the wizard jury agreed to and her magical powers reacted to her developing mood.

All she wanted was to be free like Asari, being able to run wild and enjoy life, but frustrated, she had cursed someone. Malee was jealous of the other children. In an attempt to flee herself and save her newfound powers.

The young girl developed a passion for reading because of her parents' strict parenting. They did not want their daughter to be a warrior. She was going places. The King and Queen took control at an early age and controlled her power when she first gained Xeiar abilities. The King's first attempts to keep her mind in the ancient books was at the age of six years. In a quest to free her mind of continuous studying, learning how to control her powers, and learning how to be an actual kid.

She noticed his adventurous nature and wanted to partake in new things. Asari represented something she didn't have in her life. Fun!! She spent most of the week sneaking out to go see the boy, taking a break from her studies and finally have some fun for once. An idea that Malee had dismissed on many occasions, until this fateful day when she decided to finally sneak out of the palace to go find him.

Their children had led their young curious minds to the forbidden lands, somewhere Asari never been to before and where his older brother didn't want him going. There are many powerful Xeiar creatures to be found in this area. Many wizards know to leave them alone.

The children had spent most of the evening exploring the forbidden area until a scream from the village startled them. The two youngsters, accompanied by a Quinoragoras child, looked up to the sky and seen scattering meteors falling. Suddenly, the Quinoragoras child deteriorated in front of them. Xeiar guards found them and escorted them to Grand Xesus to see the Greats. Apparently, in their quest for fun, they had destroyed a planet and created portals as creatures fled into... going to another place.

There's a little more to this destruction of planet Xirxion and it will be explained via a future episode in another series. It happened around the same time they were running around in forbidden areas.

The girl was already there, more saddened, scared, and confused, standing amid the three wizards who were humming some kind of spell.

Asari closed his eyes as a ring of smoke engulfed them from the wizards' cloaks. They were trapped between the judges now. The weather seemed to change right there where they were standing clouds, huge clouds separated them from the crowd and in a moment, they were completely in a world of their own. Clouds, lightning, and smoke were everywhere and the world around them seemed to spin too fast that in no time they were too dizzy to even scream.

VALDESMON DIMENSION

The place was dark; almost the same as being blindfolded. The pitch-black darkness almost felt tangible. He couldn't see or hear anything. All around him was what felt like walls of cold metal. The floor seemed wet; he doesn't even know if it's a floor exactly. There's nothing here. He felt like he had been locked up in a world of his own. The echo of the door closing moments ago, if there was indeed a physical door, was the only sound playing in his mind. One would have thought that it was just the darkness was it not for the emptiness of the place. There was no sound, no object; not even the sound of the wind or birds. It was just a dark, silent world of nothingness.

Suddenly, there was a little sound from a distance. It felt like two loads had been dumped somewhere. The sound echoed for a while before returning to the usual eerie silence.

ELSEWHERE IN THE DARK PLACE...

Malee woke up. Her head hurt from all the swirling. The first thing she noticed was the cold. She had nothing to cover her apart from the clothes she had worn before going to court. The darkness was extreme too.

MALEE. *Confused.* Hello. *She called nervously.* Hello. *Her voice echoed back to her.*

She rubbed her teary eyes, trying to make them used to the darkness. Nothing changed. She couldn't see a thing. She moved forward, trying to reach for anything.

MALEE. Hello, is someone here? *Nothing.*

Meanwhile, Asari had spent what he estimated to be hours running around the dark vacuum screaming and calling for help, speeding and falling in the process until every part of his body hurt. He now sat down and cried desperately.

ASARI. Hello?! *He shouted. Echoes of his voice came back to him, followed by the dead silence.* Is anyone here? *He asked himself.*

This time his voice breaking off into a desperate cry. He became quiet for mere seconds, in between the brief silence, he heard little whimpers coming from someplace in the darkness. His heart raced, his hopes of finding another living being in this hell reigniting.

ASARI. Hey! Is anyone there? Can you hear me?

Cried because he didn't understand why he deserved this; he cried because he was angry that his brother had just watched him being sent away and did nothing. But what made him cry the hardest was the fact that he was lonely, and somehow he had to live like this for the rest of his life. This was just the first day, yet he had lost all hope. Laying on the ground and trying hard to ignore the biting cold, Asari cried himself to sleep. Somewhere else in this dark universe, a scared princess was still trying to make sense of whatever had taken place, and how her life had taken a drastic change in just a blink of an eye. Unlike her friend, she couldn't even cry. She just sat down and internally cried her heart out.

It was impossible to keep track of days in this cold hell. So was it futile to try and mark the distance traveled or even assume that you could keep the sense of direction? Asari just kept on moving since the first day he arrived there. He had given up trying to scream for help here. He just kept walking, hoping that one day he would probably find the light at the end of this tunnel; literally. It was this hope that probably kept him moving, for months and months until one day when he stopped on his tracks. He had gotten so used to hearing nothing more than the echoes of his footsteps and breathing that not a single strange sound would escape his ears. He was sure that he had heard something like a whimper from a distance. He followed the voice curiously, careful not to make a sound that would scare whoever it was.

Asari followed the voice, only to hit a metal wall, forcing him to fall on his back. He now realized that the other person was in another adjacent room. There was no way of reaching her, but at least they could talk. He heard the whimpers get louder as if the girl in the other room was also trying to reach him. She reached the wall and stopped. The whimpers intensified.

He heard it again, this time not very far away. His heart raced. He stretched his hands into the dark and to his shock, he felt something.

Malee almost jumped. She felt something touch her shoulder from the darkness. She jerked, getting to her feet ready to defend herself. She was sure that there was no possibility of finding something good in this place.

ASARI. Hello? Are you there? *He asked, realizing that he had scared the person away.* I'm not here to hurt you. I – I just need your h – help. *He said.*

Malee couldn't believe her ears. The voice was all too familiar. If she wasn't in another nightmare, then this was the greatest moment in her life. So was this Kweezan's voice or Asari's?

MALEE. Asari? *She whispered back, still doubting her luck.*

ASARI. Malee?! *He shouted back in joy.*

They were in each other's arms in a warm teary embrace in seconds. None of them could believe it. The two had spent too much time alone that the moment was priceless for both of them.

That night, or so it felt at heart, they slept like they were back home in their beds. Not even the endless cold bothered them.

ASARI. Don't worry. My brother will get us out of here. I just know it! He won't let me stay trapped in here. Just you wait. He'll be here... soon.

THREE YEARS PASS

Asari, over time, has built up so much anger toward his brother and the people on planet Xeiar. His brother never came to his rescue. Malee eventually forgot about her father in hopes to survive where they were. They had to work together to survive.

Too much had changed since arriving as two scared eleven-year-olds. They had continued communicating with each other in the adjacent rooms, whom the unsure to be tangible "walls" became one room. The two had developed a bond even in the darkness. It kept them moving; gave them the energy to face the torturous days inside what Xeiarians called, Valdesmon. Nourishment wasn't necessary. It's almost like hunger was obliterated upon being banished to this place.

The duo spent each day telling stories and walking through the darkness like trying to find any other prisoner. They found none. So much had happened, but most of it had started when Asari discovered that somehow, he could bring heat whenever they held hands.

MALEENA. This is it.

She revealed that one day she woke up to a strange sight. It took her eyes a few minutes and a thousand blinks to adapt to the strong light that somehow tore the darkness apart. Asari became curious. This startled him.

The two had been working tirelessly trying to regain their magic and they were now positive of a possibility of escape if everything went according to plan.

Despite not seeing each other, the two held out their arms and blue and pink light was coming from their arms. But suddenly went out as soon as they jerked their arms away from each other. The rest happened too fast.

They practiced on their newly found powers and within no time, they were confident enough to entertain the thought of ever escaping. They were not sure of this dimension, but they knew they must find a way to get out of this hell. The Xeiar race, their people, had to pay for what they did to two innocent children.

Asari, now calling himself, "Asarios", came the loud wakeup call that he had come to get used to for the past three years. Malee calling herself, Maleena.

Asarios heard Maleena's voice. He saw metal starting to glow. Confused. Asarios's confusion over what his older brother didn't do brought a desire and promise to swear never to forgive his brother's betrayal. Maleena was also still furious at her kingdom for sending her to this place even though the guilt of sending her father to another place will always haunt her. This anger and urge for revenge was the mutual feeling behind their strongest bond.

ASARI. They aren't ready for Asarios. *He whispered back as his hand started glowing.*

The two smiled an evil, spiteful smile.

Wednesday, March 1st 2107...

Voices.

Warped lights.

Distorted faces... Memories...

THUMP!

They landed in a heap, hands entwined in a knot, fists clenched. Maleena was the first to shake off the feel of dimension travel; the underlying effects of nausea and fatigue. Asarios groaned in mocking pain and muttered something about jetlag and how inter-dimensional transporting drains the body during travel. Maleena kicked him on the rear... Hard.

ASARIOS. *He slides away from her, rubbing his behind.* Ow! Woman, Ouch! Pfft. That was rude, Maleena! I'm tired, I am. The travel makes me portal-sick. Besides, how sure are you we are in the right place?

Maleena looked up at the portal they had come through up high as it rapidly started dissolving into stardust.

They had charted a straight course from The Dark Dimensional Prison, the Orderly Realm for the bad people who seek harm on others and do outrageous acts. No hitches. No stops.

ASARIOS. This has to be it. Shouldn't it?...

MALEENA. Asarios. Are you sure the magic trail led here? Or did you just base it all on your make-believe hypothesis?

Magic trails were unseen, faded trails of magic left behind by certain Xeiars who used a lot of magic. They could only be detected by Empaths, like Maleena.

As a child, she was a scholar. She learned how to trace Xeiar magic and it became useful.

She saw these trails as wispy, floating wraiths that darted in and out of sight. So far, she had traced it to this "Isolated" Dimension, on planet Earth. Whoever this Xeiar was, she sure had a lot of power to be able to quake the place where they were imprisoned.

Asarios created a name for it.

ASARIOS. Veil Facility.

MALEENA. *Turns her head slightly looking in his direction.* Excuse me?

ASARIOS. Heh. The name I came up to name our... *He uses air quotes with his fingers.* ...home. Remember?

MALEENA. Oh, right. *Turns her head, looking straight out in front of her at huge trees in the distance and what could be a town to the right.* An interesting read I found back when I was a child. Veil Facilities were hidden, max-security prisons that were tucked away in-between pocket dimensions, unseen unless by certain, password-like spells.

ASARIOS. So, in other words, inaccessible. *Exhales a breath of air.*

MALEENA. Yes. Anyone kept in one was left to rot and die, or to be protected from enemies.

ASARIOS. Yet this Xeiar had somehow torn it out of its place and ripped the two of us out of it.

They had escaped the moment they started feeling the quakes and distortions. A rip in the darkness which pulled them through a winding vortex, making their way to this world and finally seeing Light.

ASARIOS. Now, we are on the hunt. Had we—

MALEENA. There is no hypothesis in magic. The feeling of Dark Xeiar spells is at work here... You'll see it, once I reveal it to you. *Raises her right hand and without speaking her hand shines pink.*

The male wizard can see what his friend is seeing now.

ASARIOS. I appreciate you, my dear friend. Heh-heh. Now that I can see this trail, we'll both follow and it should lead us to the one responsible.

MALEENA. Do you have any more doubtful remarks? *Seeing the look on his face and deciding to shut up.*

Asarios could be vainglorious and narcissistic, but he's rarely wrong when he made a prediction or followed a trail. And the look on his face showed that he wasn't playing this time around.

MALEENA. OK then. Let's find our mystery person and sort things out. Are you ready?

ASARIOS. Always ready. *A look of malice in his eyes as he started walking in the direction to the town. He grinned and while walking lightly caressed the runes on his palm.*

MALEENA. *She thought.* His trigger-happy move. *Following behind him.*

They immediately set a route for the nearest town. On foot, of course.

A significant amount of time passes...

It was close before they came to the end of the trail. They had stumbled into a small town, hidden by the Techy Mountains, full of rocky hills and springs that gushed from an unseen underground source.

Passing by the houses which were neat and small and the streets swept clean; its inhabitants quiet, mildly curious. They had passed some dogs who had barked madly at them, probably sensing the Otherworldly essence surrounding them. They had hurried along and cut across strange, twisted alleyways to avoid detection or harassment. You never could be too sure in a small town like this... Although mysterious, the two did not want to draw attention to themselves. They were on a separate mission than their end game.

The "wraiths", magical energy left behind, had darted in and out of reach till they got to an isolated cottage past Techy Mountains, sitting just on the outskirts.

Till they stopped, they didn't see a single soul, man or animal that so much as dared to follow the path to the cottage.

MALEENA. *She thought out loud.* Strange. Did they also sense the Dark Magic behind their normal sight?

The cottage was small. Nothing out of the ordinary. Tidy on the outside. They walked up to the door and paused, Maleena placing her left palm on the wooden door. She closed her eyes and started sensing the sort of magic that resided in the house.

If it was pure, her eyes would light up white. If dark, her eyes turned completely black. She was a walking Magic scanner.

In this case, her eyes turned so black it shone believe it or not. She immediately retracted her hand as if burnt. She made to touch him, but she placed a finger on her lips and motioned for him to hide. He was about to ask why, but the door suddenly swung open and an old woman stood there.

No time to duck. No time to dive.

ASARIOS. *Hiding on the other side of the door, he whispered.* **Deparo**.

An invisibility spell, able to disappear for seconds and longer depending on the user's power.

In a split second, he was unseen except by extreme Empathy. Those with this extreme Empathy could sense presences and follow magical trails. Those, like Maleena. She knew where he was, and discreetly made a sign for him to stay put.

MALEENA. Hello, ma'am! *In the most light-hearted and polite sounding tone of voice.*

She replied just as well, in a voice that said little. Painted her as a cheery, old woman with plenty of gaiety. The type to make pancakes and sweets anytime you visited. But could this be the person who had practically opened an invisible doorway to a dark prison? Or was a mystery Xeiar in hiding holding this woman hostage? It was plausible that…

UNKNOWN ELDERLY WOMAN. *Reacting fast.* **Iklos butish nalontis**!

She had made a daring move and repeated a not so familiar spell that she was compelled to reply.

MALEENA. **Scol–** *She reacted too late.*

The old woman drew in a sharp intake of breath, and in the twinkle of an eye, flashed a dagger out of nowhere and shoved it in Maleena's stomach. Asarios made to break out of invisibility and attack, but he saw her give a signal for him to stay put. Again.

ASARIOS. *Chortle laugh.* Heh. She's a fool. *Muttered under his breath.*

The old woman spoke then, her voice and clothes weren't of the much-revered and feared robe of the Xeiarian's.

UNKNOWN ELDERLY WOMAN. *Hand still on the dagger as she spoke calmly.* Who are you and how did you find me?

MALEENA. *Moaned silently. She was calm and relaxed in her stance.* I was a prisoner in the Veiled Facility you destroyed. You may know of it as, Valdesmon. I managed to escape.

UNKNOWN ELDERLY WOMAN. *Scrutinized her with a look of faint amazement, and replied.* I am surprised. I have no idea what you're talking about. *Spoke as if lying.*

MALEENA. I am positive you are the source. I sensed no magical essence until arriving here… to this planet. So, I'll ask you. How did you do it?

UNKNOWN ELDERLY WOMAN. *Eyes half-closed, looking at the young woman with interest.* What guild do you belong to, girl?

MALEENA. You want me to make my attack. You see your blade does not affect.

UNKNOWN ELDERLY WOMAN. Huh. *Look of confusion on her face all of a sudden.*

Asarios kept his lips sealed. He took notice and smiled.

The elder woman started to twist the dagger in deeper, but a force stopped the movement of her hand.

UNKNOWN ELDERLY WOMAN. *She yelled, something between a curse and a plea for mercy.* Lord have mercy! What grand sorcery is this?! *Her eyes widened in surprise.*

Before she could make another move, Maleena signaled and Asarios revealed himself.

UNKNOWN ELDERLY WOMAN. Great Caesar's Ghost.

Asarios had broken out of his invisibility and immediately his sword appeared in his right hand. A smile crossed his face, eyeing the elderly woman.

ASARIOS. *Chuckles.* Heh. This Caesar can't protect you.

A look of horror as the sword formed out of essence in his hand and lit up with a dark blue flame.

The wizard turned in reflex and began to raise her hand as an unfamiliar symbol shone on her head… It like Lit up.

Maleena grabbed the woman's hand, which was holding on to the dagger piercing into her stomach, and pulled it out with ease. There was no yelp of pain. No wincing.

The woman's features, frozen in shock. Her dagger turned to dust. In seconds, there was nothing left of it.

No one spoke for a while.

ASARIOS. Heh. Almost too easy, eh Maleena?

MALEENA. **Healoris.** *She whispered and her wound and clothing healed to normal appearance.* If one looked on the bright side… I would be dead right now. *Unsatisfying facial expression.*

UNKNOWN ELDERLY WOMAN. You two… *Speaking in confused and astonished.* Are what?

ASARIOS. *Eyeing the elderly witch.* The question is… What should we do to you now? *Silent laugh.*

For the first time it felt, Asarios heard Maleena snicker, as a fire lit up covering his right hand.

MALEENA. We do what mortals do to witches. Heh-heh.

ASARIOS. We burn it all. *As he started to guffaw, and his eyes burned with fiery passion pace and furious fun-filled evil rage.*

The two young wizards turned, facing the elderly witch. They jumped back a few feet and pointed their flamin' Lit arms at her cottage. The two smiling wicked and malevolent as the force of fire burned the place.

Five minutes later…

The small cottage was done. Charred wood lay around the two and pieces of personal in-door unrecognizable house items. The wizards had continued their assault then later watched the cottage burn from afar.

Neither one said a word. They simply watched in silence as the greedy flames licked the cottage to crumbs of ash and coal.

ASARIOS. She deserved it for trying to harm you.

MALEENA. *She had to look at him out of her peripheral vision and nearly blushed. But that would make her appear not so deadly. She turned, eyeing where the cottage stood.* I don't see her.

ASARIOS. There's a unique substance here. Magic, but not of Xeiar.

MALEENA. Exiled, she was.

ASARIOS. That's my guess as well. Heh-heh. I think she was well sentenced to this planet before we were sent away.

MALEENA. Well… We did learn who. What do you think, Asarios? Should we pursue–

ASARIOS. *Interrupting.* Not. *Attitude and expression changed now. He's focused solely on his mission now. He turns, facing Maleena.* We're free to leave now. Whoever she was, she's on the run now. None of our concerns. *Looks away and smirks.* We work on the plan we discussed as we were locked away.

MALEENA. I'm with you. *Sighs.* That was our thanks for freeing us. *Her eyes look where Asarios is looking.* Their trail isn't far.

ASARIOS. After we're done absorbing their magic… We'll visit Xeiar.

The two fade away, returning to Valdesmon to which they have full control to enter and leave at will now. All thanks to that mystery witch.

SATURDAY, MARCH 4TH 2107, 10:15 A.M. *(EARTH TIME)*
Planet Earth, Cattesulby Woods

Meanwhile, walking through the Cattesulby Woods before Christen appeared, Niara wondered why Akiru wanted to be alone. After so many questions and pestering, the fiery boy broke down. He shouted, turned around and threw his grandmother's name out there.

NIARA. *Spooked and has her eyes on him carefully.* Um… What does your grandma have to do with you being a loner?

The boy looked at the dirt under his feet, tightening his fists.

AKIRU. *A single tear in his left eye. Speaks softly.* Why do I have to forgive people? They're mean to me for no reason. I just… I hate people at school so… much! *He uses the back of his right wrist to wipe his face, wiping away the oncoming tears. After a few seconds, he lowers his arm back down and sighs.* I was eight years old when I heard my grandmother… *my blood* …talking about me, to my mother. *His voice breaks and he becomes quiet.*

FLASHBACK...

Akiru is eight years old. He is in his room, watching an action television series. Some gayly dressed heroes are running around fighting bad guys. A few seconds pass and he hears his grandmother's voice in the kitchen. He decided to get out of his bed, walk out of his room, and creep downstairs.

It's late and he's not supposed to be out of bed. He makes it downstairs quietly and peeks into the kitchen's double doors (the doors are cracked open). His grandmother, Mrs. Valisah H. Wellsworth, is speaking to her daughter, Mrs. Melissa Wellsworth-Skalizer.

VALISAH WELLSWORTH. Aw Sweetie, this is so not how I imagined your future. *Shaking her head.* You were *supposed* to be my 'Golden Child'. I wanted you to be something in life. I dreamed you would go to college, marry a very handsome and wealthy young man. *Sighs.* I am very disappointed that you chose *not* to finish your college education. I mean, you *ruined* your *life* to settle down with that ignorant jock!!

The two women both sigh.

VALISAH WELLSWORTH. A few years ago you just got a divorce with *that* boy's father! *She raises her voice a little and becomes a little emotional.* I raised you better than this! Why didn't you see that man's true colors sooner?!

Her daughter's mute. She continues to listen to her mother.

VALISAH WELLSWORTH. I very much saw this happening before you had a baby with that man, and then you married him! It was the most God-awful decision you could've ever made! *Calms down and sighs.* As for little Akiru... I wouldn't be surprised if he grew up and became just like his father. He runs around with his "Uncle Dante" a lot! I can't believe you put up with that. Their whole family is trouble. Dante was in a gang for crying out loud. You know the shady things Dante did in the past and I'll bet he's still doing them! *She looks at her daughter and shakes her head in disgust.*

MELISSA WELLSWORTH-SKALIZER. *She continues to be mute and rolls her eyes.* Are you finished mother?

VALISAH WELLSWORTH. Child, do not interrupt me!! *Her finger extended and pointed straight up at the ceiling. She lowers it in seconds.* Where was I? Oh, right. Well, I honestly do love my grandson, but I don't appreciate what his father did. He lied to you. He got you pregnant. And now you're divorced. I forget dear, please remind me. What do people say about bastard children? *Pauses for a couple of seconds.* Oh, right. They say that the seed doesn't fall too far from the tree. Your son will end up just like his father... and the uncle! *She shakes her head and rolls her eyes.* You know, I can't even sit here anymore. I'm all heated. I'm leaving. *She throws her right hand in the air dramatically, head facing away from her daughter.* Tell little... Never mind.

MELISSA WELLSWORTH-SKALIZER. *Shakes her head.* His name is Akiru, mother.

VALISAH WELLSWORTH. Yeah, I know my grandbaby's name! Just tell him, G'ma loves him. *Gathers her things and exits the house, leaving out the door located in the kitchen.*

Honestly, Melissa wanted to tell her mother off right then and there, but she couldn't. Partially she knows what she did in her teenage years was young and stupid. She sighed, stood up, and went to go check on her son. Akiru had been back in his bedroom for a minute now. He was in his room crying his eyes out, hands between his legs and all. He did not hear everything, but he heard enough. He discovered what his grandmother truly thinks about him. Akiru heard things he shouldn't have from a family member. His little heart had been broken.

PRESENTLY...

NIARA. *Worried.* Are you okay, now that you got that off your chest?

AKIRU. *Raises his voice.* What do you care?! *Takes a couple of breaths.* No one cares about me.

NIARA. Those things your grandmother said were so mean. She had no right to say that.

AKIRU. *Eyeing her curiously.* Are you reading... *my mind*?!

NIARA. How else was I supposed to know? I sincerely apologize for intruding on your memories like that.

AKIRU. *Tightens his fists, breathing slowly and staring at her unblinkingly almost.*

NIARA. *Raises her left hand, palm facing Akiru.* Lil' boy. You need to chill before you get dropped. *Gets defensive.* I suggest you calm the hell down unless you want to feel *more* of something else. *She lowers her left hand, looks up, closes her eyes, and then sighs.*

AKIRU. *Shakes his head.* Whatever. *Turns around, facing the end of the woods.*

NIARA. *Turns and looks back at him seconds later.* I'm trying to help you.

AKIRU. Pfft... Who says I want *anyone's* help? *Shakes his head.* Open up to *anyone*, that's just asking to be bullied and ridiculed.

The day when Mrs. Wellsworth said those horrible things to her daughter was the day Akiru's innocence and the happy smile vanished. After that, every time his grandmother stopped by to visit, he becomes distant. He goes into his room every time because that's the only place he feels at peace with himself. He pulls out his drawing pad and starts doodling. It's all he felt like doing.

Despite what Akiru's grandmother said about his father and his uncle, he still had much respect for his uncle. After his father left, sometime when he was five years old, that's all he had. He looked up to him. He loves Dante. He wants to be just like him… strong, mysterious, cool, and just totally awesome!

Nearing the edge of Cattesulby Woods, Akiru and Niara encounter the cross-human Christen.

It seemed an age since they'd passed the entrance sign in the woods, but the time it took for the fiery cross-human boy to run from one length to the other was swift and mortally unnecessary.

Akiru breathed the open, clean air as the young teen girl patted his back, peering around as she combed through her dirty brown colored hair with her fingers.

NIARA. Good job, Akiru. You've... sorta done well on controlling your emotions. *Smiles.* Let's rest for a bit.

The boy collapsed in a heap in response, taking a knee and blackening the grass with his scorching breathe.

CHRISTEN. Ah, what are you two birds doing here? Heh-heh.

The girl whipped around, blue light surrounding the palms of her hands as a teen boy holds his up in playful surrender.

CHRISTEN. I'm not here to hurt you girl. No. My business is with this mangy old wolf. *Speaking obnoxiously, ignoring the quick growl that Akiru gave off.*

NIARA. Who are you? *The blue flames grew as she waits for a reply.*

After a brief pause, the boy states his name is Christen. His eyebrows rose in expectation until the young witch reluctantly introduced herself.

CHRISTEN. Niara. Such a lovely name. It rolls off the tongue, and perhaps that's why you've stuck with her. Eh, Akiru? Heh-heh.

The wolf boy had enough.

CHRISTEN. *Enjoying a selfless laugh and relaxes himself a bit.* Ah, so sorry about not introducing you before. This is a friend of mine...

The child, full of Moxy, suddenly shifted and out from the trees a strange creature, resembling a feline species, walks out toward its owner. As the cat became a being of light and merged with Christen's pendant, the two transformed with ease into a cat that blended in as night.

NIARA. *Surprised expression and she thinks to herself.* Looks can be very deceiving.

She wonders whether this kid knew of their abilities. Akiru's secret beastly transformation might give them a massive advantage.

AKIRU. *Unnervingly, not paying the female any mind.* Christen!! *Shouts.* Quit playing around. What the hell are you doing here?! *He growls.*

MULOR. *He shakes his head, speaking to himself.* Don't even realize. In this form, I am Mulor.

AKIRU. *Breathes out.* I don't care.

MULOR. Ah, how disappointing. What? Heh. I'm not allowed to visit an old friend?

His words were met with a silent and a hard stare from the girl.

MULOR. Fine. Have it your way then. *Sighs.* A little birdy told me you two were roaming around these parts, and I knew I just had to visit you. You know how I love seeing old friends... nothing pleases me more than reacquainting with your hairy ass. *He hissed with a smile, as he riled up his nemesis.*

AKIRU. Son of a bitch!! *He swore, gnawing his teeth.*

NIARA. *Surprised expression and tone of voice.* Akiru! Do you kiss your mother with that mouth?

MULOR. *Laughing hysterically.* Of course! Ha-ha. Niara here probably hasn't seen your true self.

Akiru leaps out, unable to control himself anymore. He aims for Mulor's furry neck. Even in human form, he's quite strong and agile.

His aim is precise and he only narrowly misses, to which Mulor nervously laughs before phasing into the dirt below his feet. In a matter of seconds, and has shifted into the electric cat, a lightning bolt shoots out of the ground and into the sky above. The form of MuLit is hovering over the heroes' heads.

He lunges for Niara, prowling around her to distract and taunt Akiru, The girl corners herself in front of two huge trees where she can easily lay eyes on him. He quickly shifts his form into the water cat, Muse, creating a small wave from his body that slams down on top of her, blasting her through the trees and knocking her to the dirt ground. With shaky legs she had sent dagger spells in the cat's direction, managing to give him a significant cut before being hit by the disastrous water attack.

She stands, breathing at a steady pace, and she uses an energy shield to block its feral-like attacks. However, Muse quickly recovers and bit by bit stalks in to close the distance.

AKIRU. *Yells.* Niara!! *Shifts into half his wolf form.*

His head changed to resemble a canine's, while his claws sharpened and lengthened. The cat with water powers is giving her one hell of a fight. Her fireball manifestations are doing minimal damage to the cross-human, but then he shifts his form into the electric cat and goes after and starts attacking Akiru.

While Akiru was stronger and faster in this new form, Christen, as MuLit, has more practice fighting in close combat and soon the fire boy's furry suit was stained with mud.

Aiming at the side is always Christen's favorite. Painful, but never inflicting too much damage to kill an opponent too quickly.

The battle has only raged for mere minutes when the grass and dirt underneath them begun sweeping in circles, rising upward in little snowy tornadoes.

MULIT. What the —?! *Calls out, as the tornadoes grow stronger.*

The three teens can hardly keep themselves planted on the ground.

Niara peers through the building snowstorm, spotting a creature three times her size appear, but then shrinks to the size of an athletically semi-fit teenager's body.

NIARA. *Trying not to get swept away by the snowstorm. Shouting.*
       That's one of the hunters that the black smoky spirit
       creatures possessed!! *Storm becoming stronger.* Ahh!!!!
       Shielding her eyes. We cannot defeat this spirit before
       removing the human out of its combined body!

In the form of a silhouette teenage boy, the monster was in its weakest and most vulnerable form. It looked like a shadow, or spirit that consumed all living things in its path. The creature, carried by the wind shrank down quickly, eyes on his prize.

NIARA. Akiru!! *She shouted as debris swept past leaving a deep*
       scratch on her left arm. She clutched it, trying not to cry.

She could hold her own against Christen in cat form, but now it seemed more reinforcements had arrived. Something about the boy unsettled her; it was a feeling that made her legs shake and her skin crawl. She'd felt this once before, only in the presence of a truly dark entity during one of Itisa's combat lessons.

Akiru and MuLit, who phased back into their original selves, stopped fighting in confusion. Christen shrugged as he stared lackadaisically at the storm.

CHRISTEN. That's not me! *He exclaimed, furrowing his eyebrows at the seemingly harmless-looking boy.* I didn't give order to this assault.

AKIRU. *He retorts.* I'll never believe anything you say.

CHRISTEN. Why does it seem to be going after your friend?

AKIRU. *Rams into his nemesis, knocking him on the ground. Shouts.* How do I know this isn't a diversion or a trick?! *He asked warily.*

CHRISTEN. You don't. But it seems to be eyeing her and I don't think it's a good thing.

The fire teen turned and sure enough, Christen was right. The icy creature has conjured chains and is now swinging them towards his friend.

AKIRU. Shit!! Argh… I hate to admit when you're right. *He growled.*

CHRISTEN. I don't usually work with others, but this needs to be taken care of quick! *He cracks his knuckles.* Come on. *Turns to look at Akiru.*

AKIRU. Enough of your blabbermouth!! We can help her!

CHRISTEN. Heh-heh. *Thinks to himself, eyeing the creature in the building snowstorm.* I told him to lay low and wait. Now he'll die. *He yells, before transforming into one of his fighter cats.*

GLACIE. Niara. *The creature spoke soft, yet Niara can hear his words loud and clear in her mind.* Since the day you were there at Neirolo. I knew you could help me reclaim my original body.

NIARA. What? I can – hear his thoughts. *Quiet for a few seconds.* But I don't know how to restore you.

The icy creature lands on the ground, storm disperses. Now in the form of Glacie, he starts moving closer while swinging the ice chain at his sides.

AKIRU. *Fury in his voice and expression.* Go to hell!!!! *He screamed, shifting his form and attacking from behind.*

Glacie stopped walking and suddenly grew three times his size and easily dodged the attack, becoming a smoky entity again before rematerializing much closer to the girl. She gasped and produced a magical shield against him, struggling as the creature tries to push through.

GLACIE. My dear… I will kill every one of your minions if that is what it takes. *He muttered menacingly.*

Niara willed trees to fall, targeting the creature's form. In this way, perhaps they could beat him, but in his shadow form, there was a slim chance of catching him.

MuLit sent electric shocks in the direction of Glacies' hands, causing him to drop the chains, while Akiru comes in from the side to knock him down.

The two shifters changed their forms quickly, throwing punches on opposing sides… a strong right hook and a kick to his right hip sent the creature flying towards a nearby rock. His shadow form subsided upon impact.

With a sickening crunch, the creature's body lay limp against the sharp rock. But no blood was spilled, and a second later Glacie rematerialized the ice chains. Akiru and MuLit stared in disbelief as Glacie just stood there smiling, before swinging the chains against both of them.

Winded and injured, the two shifters glanced at each other, and at Niara who only just escaped Glacies' capture with the help of her shielding spells.

AKIRU. *Huffs.* Invincible.

MULIT. There's a weakness. *Soft exhale.*

The fire boy glanced at his former nemesis and nodded quickly, before shifting to his wolf form again.

Glacie swings his heavy chains against the dodging electric cat. He grunts as a particularly powerful wave knocks him down. The electric cat jumps to different corners, shocking his opponent from multiple different points.

Akiru joins the battle, landing new strikes to the creature's side and chest, but that only knocked him down for a second. He dodges two large swings, but could not escape the third one, falling in a heap next to Niara.

NIARA. *Whispers a healing spell, placing her hands on Akiru's bleeding head.* **Healoris.**

AKIRU. *Coughs.* Help! *Coughs twice.* You need to help Christen! I know you have more in you! *The wounded boy bit out and tries standing with the girl's assistance.*

NIARA. I'm not leaving you. *She muttered, concentrating as the wound closed.*

In roughly a minute, Akiru had been healed, but it was too late. Christen has nearly been split in half by the chains if it wasn't for focusing too much on his counterparts and not paying full attention to his opponent's attacks. Akiru loses balance but manages to stay up.

The girl's spell takes a while for the effects to kick in. She's only human and not a full-blood Xeiar.

He stood up quickly, trying to hold off black tendrils reaching out from Glacie. They seemed to swallow up the space around him... consuming everything in its path.

The creature sent icicles from the center of the large black hole which opened from his core and Niara's shield is the only thing stopping them from being skewered.

Christen tries to attack from the side, biting the creature's neck, in which black blood seeped out. Glacie doesn't appear to be weakened.

He whips up a new snowstorm and this one grows stronger and from the looks of it, soon none of them will be able to see anything.

Niara's hair swept wildly, and her feet are about to crumble. She can feel her body lifting slightly, towards the black mass.

NIARA. *Holding on tight.* Akiru!!!! Fire!! *She calls out, hoping her friend could hear her.*

She can no longer see her friend until she heard it.

A deep fire, crackling. Angry. Akiru, now a full-on wolf, gave a mighty yawp and is charging around in a huge circle around the creature. Flames unleashing from his body, surprising everyone in battle. Glacie screams in pain as the flames become too much for his icy body, causing his shadow to recede. Christen, shifting into Mu, and Niara sees their chance and sends their strongest attacks to the ice monster.

Akiru feels himself glowing as the fires created a circular ring.

It's finally time! Everything in their path is wearing Glacie down.

GLACIE. Too – strong. *Trying to hold on and summon the power to remain in the fight.* The flames... are... too strong! H – How can a human possess such power!! *He grunted, trying to stand up, but failing as the force from Niara's spells forbid him to do so.*

MU. On the count of three, give him your best shot! *He called out.*

NIARA. *Finishing her spell, lowering her arms.* One! *She started counting loudly.*

MU. Two! *He followed.*

AKIRU. Three!!!! *He screamed, sending a deep flaming ball from his palms towards Glacies' face.*

The fireball smashed into the creature and the flamin' ring shrunk, centered around him.

Akiru and the others watched as the icy Quinoragoras is being crushed in a heap as he made a barbaric yell, shattering into tiny ice pieces before the warriors.

Soon the fire was no more and Glacies' body fell, gently, in the snowflakes that cascaded down past the exhausted fighters.

The snowstorm was no more.

CHRISTEN. *Shifting back to his human form.* That was... quite wicked. *He whispered with a grin.*

Akiru shifted to his human form and looked at Christen with skepticism, but the two embraced in a nod knowing that each had secured some immunity towards each other.

NIARA. Wait! Where's – *She questioned warily, looking at her surroundings.*

Just then, the three heroes saw a teenage boy's body lying in the middle of the charred and blackened ground.

CHRISTEN. *Surprised.* I didn't think he'd survive that. Heh. Though, anything can happen in this crazy world.

AKIRU. Who's he?

CHRISTEN. *Thinks to himself.* Is he a cross-human too?

NIARA. *Frowning and thinking about her first encounter with the hunter.* Lost his possession. *She shakes her head a few times.* You will never take NikoLee away from me.

AKIRU. What do we do with him?

NIARA. He needs to be in jail for stealing rare animals and selling them.

Christen is looking elsewhere, five feet of Akiru's left, staring in the opposite direction. Seeing how one of the Quinoragoras spirits has acted alone, he begins to wonder where the others are hiding right now. He turns away from the two others and starts to walk off.

AKIRU. *Eyes glued to the hunter's body, speaking soft and calm.* Where do you think you're going? *Turns and faces his nemesis.*

NIARA. *Looks to Akiru.* Aki, please! Don't do this right now. We have to regroup with the others – *Starts sensing a strange aura in the air.* What is that?!

CHRISTEN. *Stops smirking and thinking about resuming his fight with Akiru as he watches the wizard female in confusion. Speaks low.* What are you sensing?

AKIRU. *Turns and looks at the girl.* Are – Are you okay, Niara?

Christen nudges Akiru to gain his attention to see if he knows what she's doing.

The girl has her eyes shut as she's feeling a strange power moving in on their position. Suddenly, her eyes open and shift. She starts squinting at the ground in front of them, ten paces to where the hunter's body is lying.

All three of them notice shaking.

AKIRU. *Assuming it's a creature of the same species.* Not another one. *He muttered, wondering how the enemies are finding them.*

Niara quickly turned, shouted the healing spell which completely restored the two boys stamina.

The shaking starts to grow stronger and strong winds pick up.

She's surprisingly level-headed about the situation. It felt as if there was nowhere the three of them could run.

NIARA. We need a plan! *She screamed, trying to project her voice louder than the wind.*

CHRISTEN. We don't know our enemy yet! *He replied.*

AKIRU. Well… We do know he likes wind. *He adds, placing his left forearm in front of his face.*

It was as if a windstorm had suddenly hit them, and only them.

The three warriors try to move closer to a much taller tree with a cave-like hiding area. It seemed too late as trees were swaying back and forth from the windstorm and gaining some shelter was impossible.

The wind followed them. It became harder to breathe and harder to see anything more than an arm's length in front.

Niara can feel her lungs tightening due to the thinning of the air. It's difficult breathing, alike on a ship with strong headwinds going towards the mouth. They hoped the enemy would reveal him or herself soon.

Suddenly, the feel of an invisible field closed in on them. Niara attempts to push back with her own conjured force fields, but they were no match for the enemy.

AKIRU. Grrr… *Grits teeth, thinking about a plan of attack.* Soon there won't be enough room. *He yelled.*

In seconds, just as the fighters touched backs, a powerful source revealed itself.

He stood tall and proud, in a blue robe half draped to one side of his body and from the looks of it formed from wisps of shadow.

His form was also clad in royal blue armor, but it was less and most of his body was exposed. He wore no helmet, a metallic headband around his forehead. His eyes seemed to pierce the three warriors, and they involuntarily shook where they stood.

The shield around them seemed to tighten but stopped before they felt like they were going to be truly crushed.

NIARA. *Gasps.* Who is that? He feels – He f– *Terrified of the power he's giving off.* He can't be one of the Greats that my mentor warned me never to meet.

CHRISTEN. His presence is that of …. *He whispered.*

NIARA. This isn't giving me the greatest vibes.

AKIRU. It's like the guy from before, but much, much stronger.

NIARA. *She whispers back.* I agree.

UNNAMED ENTITY. I am one of the mighty Xeiar Gods, Amras. *Responded with a smug look. He peered at the three expecting their recognition, frowning a little when he was met with blank faces.* I see you destroyed the spirit residing in an old Quinoragoras remnant… Neirolo Cavern. *Sighs.* What remarkable skills you three possess at your age. Don't worry, you haven't upset me. That particular species wreck everyone's nerves.

CHRISTEN. *Speaking out of turn, rude and loud.* Shut the shut up and state why you're here!!

AMRAS. *Shaking his head.* You three are very strong, and it would appear a lack of manners.

AKIRU. What was that?! *Mirroring his cross-human counterpart manners.*

AMRAS. Hm. Why not have a little fun challenge at destroying you. *Finished with a menacing chuckle.*

The Xeiar God spread his arms wide, summoning the power within himself. Bluish-white sparks crackled at his fingertips, whilst a black whirlpool formed at his feet. The power could be felt in the air, thickening with a stench of electricity.

NIARA. *Having experienced this power before. She stood in the sunlight, completely drained feeling on the inside. Voice trembling and speaking low.* Itisa… *She stares at the guy as her heart constantly skips a beat. Her feet rooted in the place where she's standing and her stomach has twisted in knots.* We – We have to run, but there's nowhere this Great can't track us. *Shakes head while eyeing the fearsome man.*

The two boys stood there watching, unable to feel the powerful aura this man was giving off.

The three warriors could feel the invisible cage surrounding them, fall, and they tried to look less worried than they felt inside. Niara, shaking away her fear and gaining control, readied her hands to summon spells quickly.

The way this strange man's powers are operating, it would seem that this person surely drew his strength from some super-advanced Light forces, and thus Dark might be the best way to counteract against it.

Itisa has forbidden her use of Dark spells even if there was no way to leave an impossible encounter. The effects could cripple the young child because the darkness is a whole other entity. Itisa showed her Dark spells so she can know what they are and how to counteract against them.

None of them knew whether the god could simply dematerialize and escape that way. If that were the case, ropes and force fields would do little to hold him for very long. Perhaps there was a way of trapping him so that he couldn't run.

All she needed was to weaken him, then Akiru and Christen could turn into their beast forms and come in for the kill.

NIARA. *Speaks rhetorically.* Try our best. *She readied her hands, light emanating.*

Christen concentrates his powers to the ground, transforming into MuLit. He immediately starts drawing upon energy from the sky for his lightning attacks.

Akiru prepares himself, channeling the fire deep in his core and from the Earth itself. It felt like he was summoning all the flames from the hottest parts of the planet, and brought them for his disposal.

MULIT. We will need all the power to defeat this God.

AMRAS. Ah. *With pride in his voice.* Now that you're all ready to go—

CHRISTEN. *He screamed.* Just get on with it!! *Biting out in defiance, lunging forward with a flash attack attempting to blind the god.*

The opportunity gave Akiru and Niara to run behind the god and use their best attacks respectively. However, this didn't work because the god had invisible aura shields surrounding his person and so they were hardly penetrated.

In frustration MuLit switched his form into Mulor and used shadow attacks, summoning the dark beasts that formed four-legged creatures to surround the god.

They all were in the form of Mulor and sprayed black magic from their mouths, shooting at different points of the god's exposed body.

The Great Wizard grins as he fights back, throwing them to the ground one by one using spells. Even as Mulor kept producing his shadow species, they didn't manage to weaken him in the slightest. His body hadn't wavered and he showed no signs of injury.

Mulor and Akiru exchanged worried looks before nodding in tandem and attacking with added might. The power from the shadow cat was more concentrated when it was just from him, and he hit the god with fireballs, one after the other.

They came to the god with great speed, igniting the sky and growing as they leaped through the air.

They swerved and hit the most sensitive parts of the god, but just before they reached him, the powerful protection shield would stop them in their path.

The changling started panting in frustration as none of his shadow attacks worked and when he turned to see the other two warriors, it seemed all they were doing was adding fuel to the fire for the god's humor.

Amras was indeed much stronger than anything they've ever fought before, yet there was nowhere to run. It may be clear that the god wants all three of them corpses after the fight is through.

Niara decides to fight her defense against the god's and concentrated all her might on force fields that cut through the air. They were alike shiny silver discs that sliced through, aiming at the force field surrounding the god.

AMRAS. *Speaks while eyeing the girl using her attacks.* Hm. This girl has the aura of Xeiar, but she's pure human. There's only one who could've trained her.

They made a couple of dents, noticeable by the energy-like collision sounds, and a slight marring of the force field, but promptly rebounded back the way they came.

The girl gasps as she quickly dodged the incoming force fields that were returning like lethal boomerangs. The god took this chance to implement his first move. The ground shook as he raised his power for his first spell, smirking as the three warriors desperately tried to apprehend him.

AMRAS. Petty Earth children. There's naught what you can do against my Great magic. *He shakes his head in disappointment.* No. Not even your spells witch come close to mine.

With seemingly small flourishes of the hand, the warriors all collapsed on their backs in excruciating pain.

Clutching their chests and stomachs that had been seared, they had no energy to get back up.

Their skin feels burnt and charred in debris and the rest of their body remains untouched.

Niara screamed in horror upon looking at her burnt flesh, then realized it wasn't her actual flesh. Mulor, shifting into Muse, and Akiru decided to avert their eyes to their wounds and noticed as well.

It felt like the god had cooked them, and now they were completely helpless to any spell he threw at them.

Out of all of them, Niara was the only one with defensive shields, and she had no energy to maintain them now.

The god had sent a burning spell that targeted each of their bodies. Silent and invisible, quite different from their obvious attacks.

NIARA. *Uses a defensive shield spell.* **Nieeth!** I – Won't let you hurt my friends!! *Struggling to maintain the energy shield.*

The god sends wind blades to push the girl to the ground and she goes flying. Akiru uses his speed and agility to jump and catches her before she crashed into something that might've severely injured her.

AMRAS. That was too easy, not even a slight defense from any of you. *He chuckled, cracking his knuckles as he walked towards them, his blue robe trailing like a wedding dress in the wind behind his large form.* Am I positive you three defeated the Quinoragoras spirit?

Christen lies nearest to the Great. His eyes wide open in fear and felt in his gut that he would be kicked in the side, which might cause him to wince and no sound would be released. He'll just feel weak. There would be no way Niara could heal him from the force of that attack.

Luckily, the Great just eyes him.

AMRAS. *Feels a Dark —something inside of Christen.* ...like I need to finish a job someone hired you to do. I came here because something's going on. Indeed, this had been entertaining. You, on the other hand, are not morally right in the head like those other two humans. What are you hiding, changling?

The Great Wizards right-hand starts glowing and Niara gasps. She felt he would eliminate Christen.

Just then… a huge boulder smashed right above Amras's head. The God knew it was there the entire time and turns his head to the forest, seeing people running closer. The glow on his hand disappears as it appears he forgets about the cross-human under him. Christen takes the opportunity to teleport a short distance away, thinking he'll be safe from the terrifying Xeiar God.

ZANARI. *Running closer, out of Cattesulby Woods. Shouts.* Niara!!!!

The Prince is running quickly with Capt. Sky to his right.

AMRAS. *He raises his head and sees the two people approaching.* Well isn't this interesting. The Damonarian Prince on planet Earth. *Lowers his voice.* It must be because of the disastrous weather happening near Vrec right now.

ZANARI. *Stops running, eyeing the Xeiar God sternly.* That's ENOUGH!!

AMRAS. Mind your tongue, Prince. Present the same mutual respect as your father.

SKY. He's his own man. It is you who should have some sort of respect. Fighting against children. Ah, come on man. You're WRONG!!

AMRAS. Earth human. This doesn't concern your kind.

SKY. –But you're on OUR turf!! As Captain, I am where I belong, wizard.

NIARA. *Struggling to stand.* Get out of here!!!! Zanari, please! *Tearing up and yells.* He'll kill you!!!!

ZANARI. Niara. *Looks away from the God and watches the three teens.*

A rush of wind passes in between Zanari and the kids. The prince and Cap'n try to hold on to something.

AMRAS. Something must have clouded my vision because I did not see you off Vrec. Are you here to deal with my brother's actions as – *Tenses up and loses the thought.*

SKY. What the–?

Everyone becomes baffled due to the Greats' mysterious actions right now. What could Amras be doing? Akiru tightens his fists and growls. Christen is on all fours and smiling as if he's not injured.

A silent burst is heard and the Great vanishes. He's nowhere to be felt. The wind died down and the feel in the atmosphere has returned to normal conditions.

Meanwhile, on planet Xeiar...

AMRAS. *Lands on the ground of Xesus and staring into the eyes of Magis.* Why? We're equal!! I was trying to find answers!

MAGIS. *Shakes his head.* You forget what a group vote incorporates. *Turns and walks inside the hall.*

AMRAS. *Looks behind him and exhales.* They'll see what I tried to do. But by then it'll be too late. You're on your way, I know that. *Sighs.* I shouldn't have treated you that way. *Sighs and follows Magis into the hall for counseling.*

Returning to the ends of Cattesulby Woods...

SKY. Do you think he was called back?

ZANARI. Most likely. *Grabs his left arm and massages it.* Go see if the children are okay. *Nods in their direction.*

SKY. A captain and I'm still taking orders. *He shakes his head, laughs, and proceeds to walks to the three teens.*

ZANARI. *He looks at the clouds in the sky.* If one of the Greats is here, we're doomed to whatever the threat.

This next part of the series shifts back in time to Xanpo's childhood, starting at eleven years old. He didn't always go by, Xanpo. His real name is Leisean Juhnen.

YEAR – 2088

EXT. XANPO'S HOME. THE DRIVEWAY.

An eleven-year-old boy walks all the way home with his bicycle by his side and his backpack slung to the left, half-torn. He seems bullied and doesn't care too much about it as he continues to worry about his science project the following week.

XANPO. I am going to be alright. What can be worse than being overpowered and bullied? *He soliloquized, sitting by the front door and searches his thoughts as though he was a novice interior decorator at a new job trying to impress a wicked boss.* Yes! I know what I will do. Considering how a mecha-volcano feels underrated… I know the perfect project that'll win. *He smiles with content and walks through the front door.*

INT. THE NEXT MORNING. HIS BEDROOM.

A scrumptious breakfast awaits in the morning, and he closed his eyes because it's not exactly the right morning time of day to wake just yet.

In that instant, the ground went twirling. He suddenly started shrinking, and his bed disappeared as he floated slowly like a bubble until he hit the floor. Immediately, he sees a mouse that in turn becomes big, and bigger, then it turns to a rat. Xanpo decides to flee for his life first then ask questions later. Running became impossible as his legs were not touching the ground. The rat suddenly became a balloon with a door compartment where he was locked in. At this time, he had lost all hopes of ever returning to normal. For some reason, a thought crossed his mind and he felt it all a dream. He pinched himself then shouted. He was rather pinched with the shocking reality of being inside a rat and would be killed any time soon, and suddenly felt remorse for the rats he had killed. He cried and wished he could just return to those boys who had beaten him days earlier. Anywhere but inside this rat was the best.

The insides of the "balloon" were beautiful. Xanpo, however, was scared of this than facing the demon he had read about in one book he found lying on the floor of the school's library the day before.

Leaping high to the ceiling, the balloon went ballistic around the room. Xanpo, on the other hand, was in a frantic mood; he was shouting at the top of his voice. The ride up was jerky as though he was in a traffic jam. Up and up it went – endlessly. At times, it felt like there was a change of routes, and it swerved, leaving him to hit against the soft insides of the balloon. When he couldn't take it again, he went flat, and everything became blank.

Xanpo was out for three hours, and when he came to, he woke up with a big bang. Thousand trains in a race circuit torturing the rails to get to the railway station all in his head. Noises to make the mind go mad for decades.

FADE IN! – INT. CRICKFIELD JUNIOR HIGH SCHOOL. SCIENCE LAB.

Sometimes the road is bumpy and sometimes it is not... Xanpo is never daunted by anything. Wherever the day ends, it's where exactly the sleep awaits. Long before he started living the life of a survivor, he had a home with a fireplace to keep him warm at night, a cozy bed to rest his head when night falls and when the stars would glisten in the deep dark where heavy clouds played in the starry heavens. He had a home where a mother figure lived, a fatherless household, where sibling rivalry ran afoul, and he was a child who had no worries.

It was that season of school. There was a science excursion, and everyone had to think of something to bring to the school Science Day Fair and present in front of the whole student body, staff, and parents and visitors. Xanpo was worried about what he could do. He figures he could confide in Mr. Carbinas, one of the school's science teachers.

He's an affable character at school and amiable, but who knows what he's like outside of where he worked. He wears the same thing Monday through Friday. He dresses in dark tanned khaki pants, a light-colored turquoise button-up shirt, and draped over his body a long, white lab coat. He never came to school with scruffy facial hair. He keeps himself presentable at work, looking very casual.

Xanpo wanders around Mr. Carbinas's laboratory, leaving handprints on every glass his gaze catches, as he touches and examines all of them closely.

The timid and shy eleven-year-old boy, with no worries but school work, takes in a deep breath as he feels nostalgic all over again in a big rush. The glasses, bottles, and cylinders, with the small tech he sees in the laboratory, all took him back to the regional science fair excursion his class had to participate in the previous year.

Mr. Carbinas is Xanpo's science school teacher; he's in the sixth grade. He has come to ask some questions concerning his research project.

He's continuously wandering around Mr. Carbinas's laboratory, making his way to a very old piece of machinery left unnoticed in the back corner of the classroom where no one seems to go. He starts touching and examining a very big machine when the teacher walks through the door.

Mr. Carbinas waltz's into his "invaded" lab as he sees Xanpo standing in front of and across the room from the stethoscope; staring with excitement, yet bewildered. He's visualizing the machinery with curiosity.

At first glance, he became startled upon laying eyes on Xanpo, forgetting why he came to his classroom.

Carbinas's pale silky hair down to the mane and down to his shoulders, all lit as the lab bulb shined down against it; shining gold dust to his straight hair like that of a cat in a daze. A conversation ensued…

MR. CARBINAS. What are you doing here?

XANPO. *Avoiding why he was there.* What's this 'posed to be? *Right hand extended and pointing out to the machine standing secluded from the rest of the room like an outcast.*

MR. CARBINAS. It's supposed to be a Trans-Generic Infusal.

XANPO. A Trans– What now?! *Confused and glaring at his science teacher, searching for answers.*

MR. CARBINAS. Heh. Well… I do have some time. *He walks over to his desk, setting his coffee mug on the desk, and leans on it.* Why not! *He smiles.* Ahem. You see, many years ago, an extraterrestrial being came from a whole different parallel dimension. I guess you can call them aliens. People in that decade assumed they became bored with their home. It's very inquisitive and worth researching more. Heh-heh. Too bad they're long gone. *He smiles again, but this time it's like he's trying to hide something by the look on his face.* So, a few scientists from Earth wanted to know more about life on other worlds and cross-dimensions... if there's even any out there. These aliens had created a pathway and landed on planet Earth. Earth was more than they had expected. The scientists were able to trace their whatchamacallit "pathway" schematics when authorities raided their secret base of operations here on Earth. This raid happened after they had taken off. The local authorities didn't know what to make of it. It was taken to a higher power and it would seem those certain authoritative figures forgot about it.

XANPO. *Gasps.* ALIENS!! *His eyes enlarge, showing interest.* I always believed fables and non-fictional stories aren't fake! So, superheroes and all... They ... Th...

MR. CARBINAS. *He smiles.* They didn't become wild, or they didn't cause a raucous. From the reports I've found, they weren't like your typical aliens. Never on the attack, no sir. Heh. I guess we'll never know if a human-made weapon could take them down.

XANPO. Wow... *The surprised tone of voice.*

MR. CARBINAS. Every scientist, on this secret assignment, thought together how to eradicate these strange visitors from another world. Those mysterious beings were definitely on a quest. Before their departure, an Earth scientist discovered them building a device quite similar to the replica behind you. *Pointing to the device.* Once those aliens decided to split and leave this planet, they left behind the strange machine. A few Earth scientists worked on the machine hoping to learn what it was the creatures were trying to do. Many months past, a transporting machine was the proposed outcome of this strange machine. There was a lot of damages that had been caused. The re-designing and digging into it's strange and alien hardware systems caused malfunctions.

XANPO. *Looks at his shoes and the floor, sighing.* I wish I could be resilient and unknown to whomever... Just like those mystery visitors to Earth.

MR. CARBINAS. Well... There's no way to tell what this machine could do. The scientists stopped working on it and assumed it might be their way of continuing to finish a diabolical bomb that might go off if they ever reached a certain point while finishing the machine.

XANPO. Oh... *Sad expression.*

MR. CARBINAS. *He stops leaning on his desk, picks up his coffee mug, and takes a sip.* Ah! That's good mojo. HaHaHa. *Exhales.* So, over time, I've been working on this machine by myself. I dreamt of seeing humans becoming indestructible.

XANPO. How can that become a reality?

MR. CARBINAS. Heh. Are you asking rhetorically or if we could try it out?

Xanpo stops speaking for some time, seeking solace at the moment. Mr. Carbinas stops speaking.

A few minutes pass...

He and the science teacher speak inaudibly, backing the generic infusal machine; then, at long last, Xanpo breathes out and asks to assist in the professor's continued research on the device.

MR. CARBINAS. I'm afraid I would need parental consent since you're a minor, but... There's no harm if nothing happens. *Laughs.* This thing is busted anyway.

XANPO. *He walks over and picks up wearable gear lying on a rack next to the machine.* Let's try it. I want to see cool lights.

The young child gets dressed in some scientific materials and he steps inside the machine.

MR. CARBINAS. Why not. Heh. Are you ready?

XANPO. What's the worst that can happen?

MR. CARBINAS. Listen! The moment you feel the slightest discomfort, I'll pull the plug. It's supposedly, from what I've read off the tattered notes, tampers with human's generic structure and you'll become resilient. Not indestructible.

XANPO. *Ignoring the teacher.* I'm ready!

Mr. Carbs gives him a nod and shut the door to the machine. He turns a dial to the right. The boy gives him a nod with a smile as he turns the machine on.

For a while, the machine whirs with loud vibrating sounds and within approximately twenty seconds it turns itself off.

The teacher opens the door for Xanpo to come out. He came out with a scratch on his left forearm.

MR. CARBINAS. *Gives a sad expression, eyeing the scratch and jokes.* Perhaps it did something after all.

XANPO. I guess I'm still destructible. *Laughs with both eyes closed for seconds.*

MR. CARBINAS. The good news is you'd heal quickly… Faster than normal! *A smooth liar.*

The boy gave a quick look at the wall clock.

MR. CARBINAS. Take off the prehistoric gear and go home kid. I'll see you in class tomorrow.

Xanpo removes the gear, places it back on the hook next to the machine and walks out of the laboratory. He took note of a door that was left open to the far left of the machine. It's almost like it is giving off a transcending ray of green light across the room. The boy shakes it off and exits the room. He's seeing things that aren't there.

Mr. Carbs eyes what his student was looking at and sees nothing. He looks at the door then at the machine.

The man goes to pick up the tattered notes from off his desk and reads.

MR. CARBINAS. *Reading.* … "and so one shall see a ray of light that will take them to a faraway dimension where life feels quite alternate. Humans, altered in different ways. Creatures with extraordinary abilities than what Earth humans are used to seeing." *He sighs and gazes at the door again. He says quietly.* Did he turn around and believed he'd seen something?

THE NEXT DAY AFTER LUNCH HOUR....

Xanpo made his way into his science teacher's room. He walks on, going into Mr. Carbs's office.

MR. CARBINAS. Ah, what can I help you with today? *He said with a smile.* How's your research coming along?

XANPO. I left my research notecards in your laboratory yesterday.

MR. CARBINAS. Oh, why yes you did. *He lowers his left arm under his desk and pulls a drawer out, grabbing a hold on something.* Here they are. *He closes the desk drawer and hands the note cards to the boy.*

XANPO. Thank you. *He grabs his note cards.*

MR. CARBINAS. No problem. *Smiles.* How's your arm?

XANPO. Like nothing even happened. *Rolls up his sleeves, making his arms bare for his teacher to see.*

They both gave a smile, as the child lowers his sleeves, pockets his note cards, and turns to take his leave.

As the child left, Mr. Carbs lowered his eyes and pushed his daily reading of the local newspaper aside. He gazed down at the tattered notes.

MR. CARBINAS. *Reads a new section that is legible.* "...raging on through greyed desert sands, making way to a gr... .... Kingdom where these s..ange humans ..o possess monstrous abilities, lies inside. A test will allow wh.. shall enter and be great just like the people who live beyond the gates." *Sighs.* What in the world can this mean?

That night, the eleven-year-old boy is all ready for bed. He lies in his superhero-themed bed, ready to rest his eyes.

A few moments later...

The boy is dreaming. He's inside the science lab about to exit the room when all of a sudden he is turned around by unexpected light from the very big machine. The door to it isn't latched. It's barely closed.

He pressed a button that fully opened the door and multiple colors of light rays come blasting at him, transcending from it.

The boy steps forward, going through the door and immediately the doors shut.

He found himself wandering in a faraway land. He's lost. He pinches himself to see if he's dreaming and then he screams out because of how tight he pinched his right cheek. Everything here seems to be quite bigger and / or deserted. Nothing but grey sands around for miles. He was the only one; the plants (seemingly dead and unfamiliar to what he's used to seeing) he sees are not as tall as he is and he feels the urge to run back.

Xanpo turns back and decides to run back home.

But home is farther than he thought. The more he ran, the farther the ground rolls. As he runs, his legs were going fast, but he is not moving. The recent happenings come back to him in a flash but in bits. He looks around him and everywhere looks unfamiliar, not his bedroom, not his home, not his neighborhood, nowhere he knew.

The eleven-year-old sighs and wanders off in search of shelter in the strange land. His mind has gone blank as he doesn't know what to do.

EXT. NAMORANT DIMENSION.
WASTELANDS, MANY DAYS PASSED.

With the surroundings still strange, the young Xanpo decides to struggle away from escaping his now reality. He's… Dealing with it.

Unknown to him, he is being watched by the prying eyes of young native boys the same age as he.

He sinks to the ground, exhausted already. He needs water badly and sees the gate to the city far off in the distance. It could be miles away, taking days or weeks to get there.

XANPO. I need water. *A craving so hard to get peace down his throat to cool off the sadness that burns hot in his heart, lungs, and soul. He looks ahead as he starts walking. He starts struggling onward.*

A loud cackle from a group of boys makes him snap out of his daze of realizing he'll never escape this new reality.

A short distance, past the greyed desert sands…

ZANARI. Zanit!! Pallat!! Look at him move. *Calling out to the other boys.* He looks like us, but he is not a normal boy like us. *A thought pops into his mind.* Heh. Let's teach him a few lessons, shall we? Heh-heh!

ZANIT / PALLAT. Yes!! Hee-hee. *They chorused.*

All three boys approach Xanpo and question him, but he fails to give a reply as he doesn't understand their native tongue. He ignores them. The boys, feeling insulted, and as warriors they were, they decide to show the strength of their kingdom to the poor lost boy.

Zanari goes first, holding high his wooden sword, used for practice, and hits Xanpo to the knee, and he falls to the ground.

Not what he should do, he maintains being on all fours and the next few minutes were the worst he had felt of all the bullying he went through in junior high school. A massive smack to his back, he could hear his spine make a loud, light crack. Punches flew in the air to his face and stomach from Zanit and Pallat who now took attack orders from Zanari who stood majestically by the side of the scene.

A few moments later, after Xanpo reacts no more to the beating, he hears… STOP!!

He's left alone instantly. His ribs were near broken, his right hip, mauled and clubbed to the left with bare hands. Blood seeping slowly from his head and chest, dying was the only escape he sought. After all, he was beaten and left to die.

Days pass as each moon died for day to come…

The human eventually wandered away from his death bed and into the desert wilderness where he searches for refuge to the kingdoms gates. In his mind, he is bent on traveling to the city through the city gates.

Xanpo feels better, and he continues to find a way into the city's gated community he saw some Earth days ago.

Forty minutes later...

He eventually makes his way to the gate and sees some people around the entrance. On getting there, he notices the same people he meets at the gate are the same people that beat him to meet the creator. Another shocking revelation, Zanari was nobility. Little wonder why he was standing and giving orders that almost killed Xanpo.

In the Namorant Dimension, on planet Vrec, the planet looks like
a wasteland upon arrival. If a person focused, they would find
the king's palace as well as civilization. The palace, in actuality,
is the entire planet, but it's in one place, located on the outskirts.
Long ago, a Xeiar wizard, who was on good terms with the King,
created the outskirts on the planet to appear as an endless illusion.
This tricked foreigners and stranded outsiders who believed that the
outskirts were a big place and that the entire planet was a wasteland.

EXT. THE DAMONARIAN KINGDOM – CITY'S GATED ENTRANCE.

XANPO. *Inaudibly to himself.* I must pass through the gates. I must find a way to know where I am, and seek a way home!

ZANARI. Hey!! *Child tone of voice so impeccably stern.* Stop there! What do you want again, stranger?!

XANPO. I am Xanpo. I want no trouble. *Hands out in front of himself in a surrendering fashion.* I just want to know where I am, how I got here, why I am here, and how do I leave this place! I... *He speaks in a hurry without pausing to take in a breath.*

ZANARI. *Smiling crookedly on the left, he interrupted him.* I have no answers for you. I ask the questions and give the orders around here. Now leave my sight! You shall not be granted entrance into the city gates!

XANPO. *Lowering his arms down to his sides.* Before you put in more effort to throwing me back to wherever I came from, would you please just tell me where this is?

One of them, blind-eyed and puffed in the tongue waved him off and spoke harshly.

UNNAMED VILLAGER. *Speaking loud.* Welcome to planet Vrec, home to the Damonarians. You're in the Namorant dimension.

It feels like they had another victory over him. They all gave a wild arboreal laugh, and Xanpo went numb. He wanted to stop dreaming.

After being denied entrance to the city's gated community, Xanpo wanders off into the wastelands, the only place he has access to.

The wild is green, dark, and filled with heavy gases. And unlike being watched on cable television, he experiences this first-hand. Hissing sounds of weird, odd crawling serpents at day, shaking dead forest tree leaves at intervals and the hunger that speaks to him to just jump off a cliff to end his life coupled with monstrous roars at night. This all, quickly, gotten him adapt to his environments.

Surprisingly, he enjoyed the wild; he finds out intuitively which leaves and fruit is edible or not. He learned how to hunt for food and protect himself stealthily from his attackers in defense and his prey in the offense.

The day of the stone god, as gathered by Xanpo from little learning of the native language from miles outside the city's gated entrance. Possibly it was a worshipped stone god or not; it's all he could gather from the laid out pieces of stone. Presumably, the area he trekked through was an old battleground and the God statue was destroyed.

Hours pass and he encounters a strange person far into the distance who's native to the villagers beyond the gated community. Looks like the mystery man was out on a hunt.

Speaking of a hunt, the pains in Xanpo's stomach erupted once more.

The human teen goes in search of the day's meal far from his tent deep into the wild, to a place he has never been.

Finding trouble luring out water creatures at the darkened lake, he stumbles across the strange person.

He kept an eye on the figure, who is all strange and eerie. The man, the Caucasian appeal of an Earth male, thoroughly browned dark, as he was tanned by the sun's heat. But oddly enough, Xanpo has never seen a Sun similar to Earth's for the entire time he's been on this planet.

They both stood apart from each other, with the man in torn shorts and a metal chipped, battle-scarred knife in hand.

With a coarse voice that imitates a crocked frog's croak. It was apparent that he was mean, tired and has been alone for a very long time. His dark-shining hair struggled at edges out of not being combed for years – obviously. On his back was a backpack with all his essentials… a bluntly-looking, but sharp spear poking out of his bag from both ends.

Before seeing Xanpo, he was battling savages on the side of the stream for his "sport". There was blood on his person, but not from himself. Xanpo thought from a distance. He came up with a theory… They probably wanted to overpower him for thinking they were higher in numbers; so he must've killed them all in a rush. There's a dark smile on his lips.

XANPO. *He thought questionable.* All that for his hunt – A fish?!

EXT. TIME JUMPS ONE YEAR – 2089

He has grown into a strong young man, and as usual, he takes his daily walk to the city gates, but this time, he is in the company of the loner warrior he became (sort of) friends with some months ago.

On the way to The Damonarian Kingdom, two hear grunting. The sounds of battle are near.

The two turn to look at each other and rush to where the noise is coming from.

Making their way near the area, seeing the kid warriors, the same from a year earlier, were in a fight, Xanpo intuitively decides to help them.

The elder warrior watches before going to assist.

Their opponents, five gray beastly creatures not from the planet he's on now. The vortex/warp hole, in which the creatures traveled by, was still slightly open in the grey desert sands.

The lone warrior, seeing the whole fight, couldn't wait to get his taste of blood too so he joins in.

The eldest dashed to the fight with no invitation and swoosh!!! His ancient and beat-up sword went against one of the creatures' neck.

They were of strong elements, stronger than iron and rocks put together and his sword bounced back. Xanpo and the warriors put forces together and fought tirelessly, but are still overpowered by the brute force. The creatures swung their heads and tails in unison.

UNNAMED LONE WARRIOR. I'll help you, kids!!!! Stand back!! *Speaking in their native tongue which he has also taught Xanpo expressly.*

ALL THE TEENAGE BOYS. *Speaking all at once.* Huh?!!

The warrior tears his shirt and his quads start becoming bigger and bigger. The atmosphere becomes windy and there are lots of black and blue hues all over his body... like dust. He's at this point covered in fog, and as the mist disappears, the escape of the mist reveals a powerful beast standing on twos with long, sharp claws on both hands. He snorts and roars.

UNNAMED LONE WARRIOR. *Grizzly and deeper than the usual tone of voice.* I'll take care of these beasts!!

In a flash, he dashed into the cluster of beasts that surprisingly waited for him. They were growling all through the ordeal. Their fight feels like a powerful God-like ruler falling with other gods fighting for supremacy.

The clouds darkened unusually, and the boys steered clear as to not get caught in the apparent clash of titans.

He smashes his right claws into the middle rear of one of the creature's head, and he knew it was its weak spot. He did the same to the other, and the last of the three-bit him in the stomach, ripping out his insides. The boys gasped. But there is still a fight in him!

With a tremendous roar and massive bang, he hit one of the heads of the last beast with a lightning bolt. It dies from the blasts and the warrior writhes in pains, but he smiles and gives a thumbs-up before falling.

PALLAT. How did you learn how to fight like that, and why did you risk your life for us?!

Pallat's question goes unanswered. To Xanpo's right, he noticed the wormhole closing.

UNNAMED LONE WARRIOR. Be safe, Xanpo. *His breaths in and out one last time and life leaves his body. His eyes stare unblinkingly to the sky above.*

XANPO. *Feeling loss for his first mentor in a foreign place.* That's how we do it where I come from too. I told him that when I met him after being thrown to the curb by your lot. We helped each other... For months.

ZANIT. You managing to be alive this long surprises me. *Shakes his head once in amazement.* Where are you from?

XANPO. I am from America... planet Earth. That is what I have been trying to tell you guys all along. I am lost. I have been trying to find my way home or at least find a place to belong.

PALLAT. Hmmm. *Speaking royally.* I see what you mean.

ZANARI. …and why you were in such a hurry to get into the gates the first time we saw you. We didn't think you needed to know where you were, but we aggressively attacked you based on our natural nature. *Sighs.* My father… King Oanayi gave me a lot of training at that time.

PALLAT. He must be of noble blood. *Nods.*

ZANIT. Or not. *Staring at the human warrior disbelievingly.*

XANPO. Umm, thank you. And no, you're right! I am not nobility.

ZANARI. Only those of nobility can tell if someone's of royalty. *He laughs and a second later he has a change of heart.* Thank you for coming to assist and helping me and my warriors. *He nods.* I appreciate you… and the fallen Damonarian warrior. Your friend will not be forgotten. Come. You may now pass on through the gates. My father will want you to join our ranks.

EXT. FADE OUT AND CUTS TO THE NEXT SCENE – YEAR 2092

This next adventure exploring Xanpo's childhood speeds a few more years into his teenage years. He has just turned fifteen years old. He hasn't left this strange place since. He's now trained in the Damonarian way and knows some of their moves, skill-sets, and strategic abilities. However, he doesn't possess a transformation like the others.

He's best friends with Prince Zanari. Zanit and Pallat have grown apart and are now working in other fields in the gated community. He's learned that he's in the Namorant Dimension and that ten planets orbits Sol Moon, the numero uno moon in this dimension.

Xanpo and Zanari came across a Xeiar witch and were recruited by her. Taking them to planet Xeiar, using her magnificent spells. She taught them new tricks.

On a trek through the mysterious Crayos Forest, Itisa, the witch, told Xanpo and Zanari why she was away from her homeworld. She was placing Transporter Roons (a device capable of teleporting to and from different worlds and possibly dimensions) and trying to cover up these savage Quinoragoras creatures who roam through worlds attacking innocent people. Luckily she found out that a group of them were killed.

At the age of sixteen, he agreed to help Itisa track down monsters who were in hiding in other worlds, mainly Quinoragoras. He has been spending time on planet Coroth with a few local new friends he's made. He became friends with sorceress Crystalia, Itisa's protégé, whom he met on planet Naoth. Xanpo made friends with some unusual human-like people over the past six years away from Earth. With that, he's also made enemies and learned terrifying truths. For instance, he discovered Itisa has a powerful twin and devastating events she's been through with her blood.

He's seventeen years old right now. Xanpo has landed on a new planet. He's searching for clues leading to the whereabouts of his newest mentor, Itisa.

Where could she have traveled to and why does she disappear often?

Far away from Earth, there's a one-man expedition exploring a distant planet called, Devina.

The spaceship landed, and one person exits the craft. Walking slowly, he's become mesmerized by the planet's all too familiar atmosphere.

Devina's atmosphere, its' chemical composition, although heavier than the one of Earth, is still breathable. However, for now, the planet reveals itself as a dead, dark barren world. Only seventeen years old, Xanpo assumes there are different, more welcoming places on this planet so he continues onward. He starts to become absorbed in new, arising fears of exploring such a strange silent place.

After an hour, he spots an entrance, in a mountain. It looks like a tunnel. Even though deep down in his gut it is telling him not to check it out. He pursues his human instinct and goes inside to explore.

XANPO. What for? *His conscience spoke.* It's just a hole in a mountain. Of natural origin. Do you want to risk having an accident? Being trapped, or something like that? You're human!!!!

He shook away all negative thoughts and persisted on his clueless quest.

He's walking so slow…

XANPO. At this pace, I can go there fast and quick and see if something is interesting. And if so, then, Prince Zanari's father and his troops will welcome me upon discovering ancient secrets I've uncovered.

He enters the tunnel and in a glimpse of a second… everything went dark. But of course, he had a lamp on his person.

It seemed like a common tunnel at first, but the galleries were homogenous.

XANPO. Almost as if someone dug them. *He thought.*

After walking a few minutes without finding anything, he decides to go back. As soon as he turned, his heavy foreign backpack hit one of the tunnel walls, making a metallic sound thundering through the narrow passageways. This was a surprise.

Finally, a light shined down a gallery and he decided to make that left turn. Within a few seconds, a stone gate fell from above and closed behind Xanpo. He's locked in a small room, feeling more like a cage. He started screaming, in a panic, as gas starts to fill the enclosed area around him. He went ballistic, pounding on the stone wall in front of him and eventually fainted.

Sometime later...

Xanpo wakes up in a bed, more closely resembling an operating table. His eyes move across the small room, seeing its walls doused in whitish but murky grey paint-pigment. Maybe it's painted, maybe it's not. He's not wearing the external gear making up his Damonarian armor at the moment. The weapons he was given, by a Damonarian trainer, is sitting over by the entrance. There's a garment placed over him, but it's not a robe. He is wearing something else, something unfamiliar. A purple simple outfit, from neck to toe with a strange symbol in the center. As he gets out of the bed, a big red light, on the ceiling starts blinking in two-second flashes. The room's floor is attached to a clever alarm and equipped with an invisible camera.

A few seconds later...

The stone door slides up, opening itself and the most unexpected, horrifying creature that Xanpo ever saw walks in. Eyes wide open and in complete shock, Xanpo's eyes become locked on the creature like a predator ready to take out their prey.

It's in the form of a mutant humanoid. His or her face is an endless world of things. Organical parts, realities, accidents, aberrations... all out of place. This makes up the creature's external anatomy. A chaotic mess…. And so was his skin and limbs.

The humanoid finally spoke with a faint, but possible smile it had slowly managed to do in the context of his state.

UNNAMED CREATURE. Hello, my Earth friend. *Pauses and walks further into the room with its hands behind its back.* Welcome to planet Devina, the Quinoragoras's shall soon rule here. *It stops walking and looks into the humans' eyes.* I see you are... mesmerized by my... unusual aspect. It shall be explained.

The creature continues to walk past tables and through a doorway Xanpo had not seen earlier.

UNNAMED CREATURE. Come with me. *Going through the doorway.*

Xanpo obeys and follows the alien. After stepping out of the room, he was no less surprised when he entered a big hall. It's an extension to the previous room.

UNNAMED CREATURE. *He turns and nods at the human.* Welcome to my laboratory. My name is Dextorey, and I'm a scientist. I can speak your English language as well as other dialects fluently because I've been studying many worlds.

The surrounding division is a complex biotechnological room. The walls are filled with small tubes and pipes, pumped by liquids with different colors. In the center, there's a computer. Xanpo immediately realized that all the small tubes and pipes were sending the liquids to several different tanks, organized in two big rows. Inside those tanks, experimental creatures are waiting to be awakened.

DEXTOREY. *Hands still cupped behind his back.* Several attempts of specimens on different worlds found as you may refer to as, dead. *He nods at a tank to the left.* In this tank, for example, a fusion between a humanoid and a rat.

The creature's eyes closed and asleep in the liquid. It's face, a frightening fusion between a rat, and a man. In another tank to the right of that one, there's another different humanoid. This one much similar to an Earth human, but he has three eyes, four legs, three arms, and every last one all deformed.

On a half table further across the room, there's a dissected being that looks something between green-skinned humanoid and a wolf-ape like creature.

DEXTOREY. This one is a... Damonarian. *The word sounding as disgust upon leaving his mouth.* I see you are... surprised. Found that one a while ago. It's new. Poor thing was already dead, young Xanpo.

XANPO. *Surprised.* Huh? *Head jerked upright, staring at the creature questionably.* H– How you kn–

DEXTOREY. Yes, I know your name. I've quite a lot of knowledge up here. *Pointing at his skull for a few seconds.* And with it, comes a lot of... power.

The lost human, in mind and everything else, looked at Dextorey questionably. He realized the scientists' being was a mutant entity in itself. The combined experimented creature in tanks, all similar to him. The only difference is that he was more alive than ever.

He has two eyes, indeed, but they are of different origins. The same was happening with its teeth. Part of his skin was, in a disgusting manner, breathing in and out, like a reptile, or a frog. And other parts had hair.

DEXTOREY. Your silence says a lot, Earthling. And also asks a lot. *Exhales calm-like.* Indeed, in my laboratory, I aim to produce all sorts of wonderful beings. I believe I have achieved high levels in my research.

XANPO. *Speaking out of turn.* And what do you hope to achieve?

DEXTOREY. *As if he didn't hear a question being asked.* There's a fiery passion to every last organism across the three dimensions. *Licking his lips satisfactorily.*

While listening to these words, and traumatized by what he had seen, Xanpo's first reaction was to attack Dextorey. In a very human, but a violent way. Dextorey gestured and this made Xanpo not attempt anything. He moved as if to say he was expecting the lone human to try something foolish.

DEXTOREY. *Eyes looking at a certain chemical tank at the moment.* Let's not be brainless. I understand what you feel. All this, for sure, comes as a shock. But... on Devina, we are beyond subconscious moral restrictions. And, regardless of all that you saw, I am willing to give you something...

XANPO. *Paused, looked at all the experiments surrounding him, and then replied.* What... something?! What are you building around here?! *Pausing as he looked around, observing all the experiments that were happening around him.*

He, suddenly remembered himself to ask an important question. Probably, one of the most relevant at all.

XANPO. Why do all these creatures seem to have origins from Earth? *He thought.* There can't be more planets in Namorant who resemble humans from Earth, can there?

Indeed, Xanpo's questions were logical. If they lived on different planets, why all species seem so familiar? Yes, Dextorey was an aberration, but still... he moved and operated as a human. He's not human though. Even within his mutant body, his reptile tail crept along behind him as he spoke.

DEXTOREY. *Responding.* Why this, why that... You are too young and too bright to be a hypocrite, young warrior. Everything that's around us intellectual beings, works in a way to find more new possible venues. To experiment, and through that, to gain knowledge to and for future endeavors.

Regardless of how disgusted he was, towards what he saw, within his inner self he was forced to agree. Disgusted, yes, but... fascinated.

DEXTOREY. And, throughout my advanced technology, I could see lots of things within your mind. It is like... the Gods sent you here to make you better.

XANPO. What... What did you see?

DEXTOREY. You tell me... As you now understand, due to my knowledge regarding biological mutation, I can do lots of things. Everything...

XANPO. And what does that have to do with me?! *Voice strong.*

DEXTOREY. Seek into yourself... You know how it works, inside the regime. Do you want to be the eternal... non-warful human?

XANPO. Hm. I'm still just a kid. They will give me respect, in time.

DEXTOREY. Not if you continue to remain in Namorant. *Shakes his head twice.* No, they won't. Why are you here, in the first place? It will never change. It's not about who you are. It's who you know.

Xanpo, young, but not stupid, even within the few minutes, started to think about what Dextorey was telling him. In his mind, he knew he wanted something more... something for himself. Something forever.

XANPO. *Looks away and sighs.* Maybe you're right. *Locking eyes with the alien.* What can you offer me? *He asked.*

DEXTOREY. What does every human being want.... To be stronger?

XANPO. Heh. Not every human being wants that. I, for sure, want to be strong... So I can... Be me... And lead... And decide for others.

DEXTOREY. As I foresaw you were the intelligent individual for this new experiment I've been concocting. *Claps his two hands together.* So, let it be done. Come with me.

XANPO. *Follows the creature to another examination table.* Are there any side-effects?

DEXTOREY. No, of course, there isn't. You'll be... strong.

The scientist sent the foreign human to a bio-technical table which raised and enlarged into what looked like a closet. Once inside, Xanpo was immersed in a white liquid. This made him sleep for a while.

Twenty minutes passed...

When the liquid dried out, several numbers of rays went through him. The tubes, connected to the deceased Damonarian warrior, started to flow liquids into Xanpo. The molecules making up that lone warrior was no more. There was soon nothing left inside that tube.

Fifteen minutes later...

The liquid was all gone and the closet opened. Xanpo steps out, feeling different than a human. He tested his new strength, lifting a circular tube to the ceiling. He placed the tube down and even noticed his senses were highly improved. They were heightened. He was impressed by these new abilities.

Everything was all right for the first few minutes, but all of a sudden, Xanpo wasn't feeling so well.

XANPO. Ah! *Holding his midsection.* How come... Ah!!! *Screams out due to the new pain he feels.* All the species here... Ah!!!!!!! *Falling to the floor in immense pain.*

Dextorey just smiled, watching the newly evolved human writhing around on the cave-like floor. He didn't reply to him.

Suddenly, Xanpo soon realized what was wrong with him. This pain. He has seen it before... At the Damonarian Kingdom during training with Prince Zanari. The Prince... He has trouble mastering... His transformation unlike the others of his kind. That was it!!

Xanpo's skin was becoming darker, thicker, and lots of grey hair covered his body. Some kind of putrid leaked out from his newly opened pores as he went through the Damonarian transformation process.

The Human-Damonarian, both confident and angry, and also, fascinated with his abilities, approached Dextorey and thanked him before he left the tunnels. Xanpo could control the transformation for some reason.

Was it due to the Quinoragoras's controlled experiment? Who knows?

Hours passed... Xanpo was long gone from the alien scientist's hidden workshop and away from planet Devina.

Dextorey walked into his laboratory and gazed into a thick glass tube, eyeing a complete replica of the warrior Xanpo. The being in the tube lies asleep, features all the same just slightly off.

The alien chuckled as the scene cuts to black.

YEAR – 2095

Xanpo traveled back to the "Isolated" Dimension with a sorceress friend, Crystalia. The two separated because she wanted to view some of Earth's wonders and see how human beings were different from human beings in Namorant. They're the same physically and internally, just some features are different, like special abilities and skin-pigments. He also had other intentions. He was somewhere on the east coast, north of South Carolina and he saw a discreet flyer hanging in a subway station located near an unclaimed district. He became intrigued and went to check out the off-the-wall location somewhere underground. He had to test out his otherworldly skills.

An "off-the-maps" caged fight club, as it was strictly illegal, was in a city where lots of tourists happen to go.

There was a small round hall with a bar counter and a stage at the center. The stage was a square boxing ring with steel cage blocking escape. It's surrounded by rings of benches, commonly referred to as the VIP section. Spectators had already filled the section, and those that had not been so lucky to get a seat were struggling to find a comfortable place to stand with a clear view of the ring.

A muscular man dressed in a black suit was at the counter collecting bids from a part of the crowd who were willing to bet on their favorite fighters. There were a few murmurs from the crowd. They couldn't hide their anxiety and excitement. On the right side of the ring was a huge steel door locked by a thick rusted metallic chain. Beyond the door was a dark tunnel that led into the pitch-black nothingness; "the chamber of warriors." Outside this tunnel was a path leading straight to the rings. A table with two seats lay beside this path, and two men sat there, one of them holding on to a microphone that had been mounted on the table.

The two gentlemen kept glancing at the tunnel in anticipation. Their excitement equaled that of the noisy crowd behind them. Suddenly, one of the men looked at the tunnel and his face lightened up.

UNKNOWN ANNOUNCER. *Broadcasting his voice to all corners of the room.* Ladies and gentlemen, the moment we have all been waiting to see! Our first fight is ready to begin! *He paused for a moment to allow the cheers from the crowd to calm down.*

Suddenly, the spotlight moved from the ring to the tunnel, revealing the first fighter of the day; a young slim and toned man. He jogged into the ring and somersaulted, gloating his martial arts prowess.

UNKNOWN ANNOUNCER. Xanpo... Ladies and gentlemen!! *The announcer's voice shooting through his mic and booming from the speakers.*

A part of the crowd cheered, but their efforts were quickly drowned by more wild cheers as another fighter emerged from the chamber, springing towards the ring at lightning speed and stopping right in front of Xanpo, who was just landing from one of his show-off stunt jumps.

The bell sounded and the two young men faced each other.
Dante watched as Xanpo jogged around him, fists clenched.
He didn't move. He waited for Xanpo to make the first
move, and he did. Xanpo's fist came flying, aiming for his
jaw. He moved his head slightly, missing the blow by inches.
The rest of his body remained intact. He watched Xanpo
calculate his next move, obviously motivated by the first
attempt. He stood still, his fists clenched still. Xanpo jogged
around him, waiting for an opportunity to get his opponent
off guard. He circled him till he was completely behind him.

Quickly, he aimed a flying kick aimed at Dante's head. This
time, he turned swiftly and caught Xanpo's foot mid-air
using his left arm, leaving him to float awkwardly in the air
for a moment. Dante's right fist was ready to go. Quickly, he
aimed for the helpless man's ribs, feeling his biceps vibrate
as the powerful blow connected with Xanpo's chest. The
martial artist fell with a thud, his head hitting the floor so
hard that the crowd fell silent for a second.

Dante stood his ground, panting and waiting for any sign of
spirit from his opponent. Xanpo lay on the ground groaning
in pain, holding his chest. The referee quickly entered the
ring and signaled for the fight to end. Just as the ref's hand
was about to go up, Dante fell to the stage.

UNNAMED ANNOUNCER. Wow! That… was… Epic!!!!
          He yelled, sharing to the awe of the spectators. It looks like

our ninja will be out of the rings for a long time. It looks bad for him.

UNNAMED COMMENTATOR. It's nothing. *He added.* It will only hurt when he breaths. *He finished on a light note, much to the amusement of the crowd.*

Next to the ring was Sky, a young military recruit. He was slim and a bit toned; features that greatly contrasted to his opponent, Madin, a huge sumo wrestler. Sky looked like a mosquito in contrast to the huge guy. Sky spent most of the first few minutes of the round making quick moves, throwing powerful blows to Madin, who seemed unbothered as he tried to grab his opponent in vain. Sky was encouraged by these first minutes, he even seemed to enjoy dodging the huge arms and then quickly throwing a blow. Madin, who did nothing to protect himself or even attempt to attack Sky was slowly becoming irritated by Sky's cunning tactics. He turned and raised his huge arms. The crowd knew what that meant and they went wild. This was his killer move, what had come to be famously known as the Madin Hug. Slowly but steadily, he approached Sky, his arms spread and his huge body leaving little room for Sky to dodge or escape. Alarmed, Sky started retreating towards the ropes, trying hard to calculate a way of evading the "hug".

UNNAMED COMMENTATOR. Oh no! There is no getting away from daddy this time. *He laughed.*

Madin closed in on Sky who was now kicking and throwing blows frantically. Madin smiled.

UNNAMED ANNOUNCER. And now he has his prey
trapped, let's see what the big guy has planned.

The people were now on their heels. This was their best
part of any Madin fight. He was unpredictable. Sky saw the
gigantic fist coming to him. He quickly dodged, avoiding
the hit but hitting the ground nevertheless as a result of
the impact. Quickly, he sprang back to his feet, aiming an
uppercut directed towards Madin's chin. This time, his fist
was caught just before it could connect to its target.

MADIN. Not so clever now, huh? *He grunted, twisting Sky's
arm that he held like a little handle.*

Sky kicked the big man's groin to free himself. This only got
Madin angrier. Using his free hand, he landed a heavy blow
on Sky's unprotected head. Blood splattered on the floor
followed by Sky. The referee jumped in the ring and stopped
Madin, who looked ready to add another blow to his victim.
The crowd cheered as Madin made his way out of the ring.

UNNAMED ANNOUNCER. Ladies and gentlemen,
there have been two winners today, but as we all
know there is only one fighter who will face our
champion, Jeffery. Ahem. Let's see who among
these two has the balls to challenge the undisputed
king of the ring!

Xanpo was already in the ring, jogging, and waiting for
Madin, who seemed to take his time as he walked calmly
from the tunnel.

UNNAMED ANNOUNCER. Who will it be, the crafty Xanpo or Madin the Mammoth?

Time elapsed signaling an hour has passed in-between these two parts...

Madin stepped into the ring and the bell went off. Xanpo made the first strike; a swift double-tap on Madin's throat, choking him for a moment and forcing him to take a step back.

XANPO. Ridiculous. And to think... you... were the champion before this new guy I've never met. Pfft. *Shakes his head.* That was a quick move which could've easily been countered, big guy.

He took advantage of the stunned Madin to send a series of quick blows on his jaws. Madin tried to block the fists but Xanpo was way too quick; dodging and striking unexpectedly. Madin retreated to the ropes, wiping the blood off his lips. Xanpo stepped back, a look of triumph written all over his face.

XANPO. Come on, Papa. *He ridiculed.* Tired already?

Madin staggered away from the ropes. He looked startled. Approaching Xanpo, he threw his first blow of the round. Xanpo ducked, leaving his opponent to totter back to the ropes. He prepared to counter Madin's attack. Madin was wiser this time though. He had anticipated Xanpo's move and was waiting for him.

He turned from the ropes just in time to grab Xanpo by the neck and lifting him high. Xanpo struggled to free himself but Madin's hand was like a vice grip. He kicked and slapped but nothing worked. Madin threw his opponent effortlessly to the floor like a sack of cotton. Xanpo rolled to the ropes, taking time to regain his breath. His eyes had turned red in rage now. He leaped back to his feet and attempted a fly kick but this only landed him in the hands of Madin again. This time, Madin's fist connected with Xanpo's chest, sending him to the ground with a thud. He coughed and blood came from his mouth.

XANPO. You are going to pay for this you bastard. *He growled in anger.*

Madin had now turned to appreciate the cheering crowd. Xanpo jumped to his feet. He charged at the unsuspecting Madin, using the ropes to propel him like a catapult, then aiming at his bleeding jaw, sent a powerful fist straight to the injured area.

Madin froze for a moment as if waiting for the impact to land before finally falling on his knees. It was Xanpo's turn to brag to the spectators now. He paced around the ring circling Madin who was struggling to get up. He waved at the crowd happily. Too happily that he forgot about the fallen guy, who had now gotten up and was waiting for him to turn. He did; only to be met by a powerful right jab from Madin, closely followed by a hook right into his face that sent him straight to the ground. He stayed on the ground motionlessly.

The referees were inside the ring in no time. Madin was going to face Jeffery! The Club's champion. Bids were placed and people waited eagerly for the final fight of the day.

Jeffery doesn't have a military background like three of the others. He has a slim body and has toned features. Most fighters who got into the ring with him underestimated his physical appearance and ended up leaving in disgrace.

Time elapsed signaling an hour has passed in-between these two parts...

He looked cheerful as usual, waving at the crowd and performing stunts to show off his moves before his rival for the day arrived. When Madin finally got into the ring, with a small bandage on his left jaw, Jeffery was quick to notice it.

JEFFERY. Did you just come from the doctor's friend? *He laughed, making sure that he was audible enough for the spectators.*

Madin remained silent. The bell sounded.

Before the sound of the bell had died down, Jeffery had already thrown a jab at his jaw, removing the bandage to expose the bleeding bruise on his face.

Madin bellowed in pain and took a few steps back, wiping off blood. He looked stunned. Before he even had a chance to dodge, Jeffery was in the air, raining punches on the gigantic man's head. Madin retreated.

JEFFERY. Seems like this mammoth is a chicken after all.
   He gloated.

The champion started jogging, his eyes fixed on Madin. He gave him time to recover from his startled stance then approached him in quick dodgy steps. Madin tried to follow up on Jeffery's movements but his big body couldn't move in such speed. Before he knew it, Jeffery had performed a high kick straight to the injured jaw. The pain was almost unbearable. Madin was trying hard to remain calm. He needed to observe Jeffery prepare for his next attack. This he did.

Jeffery was now confident of his victory that he let his guard down. He came charging at Madin. Madin saw Jeffery's fist and blocked it, using his left leg to anchor his weight as well as the impact of the strike. Jeffery bounced off the big guy like a tennis ball and fell on his back. Surprised, he got up and tried the move again. This time, Madin dodged the fist then quickly grabbed Jeffery's arm and sent him falling headfirst. Madin did not give him time to recover. As soon as Jeffery struggled up, Madin was on him, sending a punch right to his jaw, his skin breaking at impact. Two more punches and Jeffery had bruises on both sides of his jaws.

MADIN. *Looking up at the limb fighter, seeing how helpless and frowned.* Your era ends today. *He said and let go of Jeffery who fell back faintly.*

The champion surprised everyone, using his free leg and jammed it into Madin's kneecap. He rolled to his right, forced his body up and used both feet to kick him to the mat.

UNKNOWN ANNOUNCER. Whoa!!!!! Seems like we
have our champion ladies and gentlemen.

As the audience started their cheers with thundering
applause, police dressed in black and grey, camo-colored
clothing flooded inside the building with handheld
flashlights a blazing.

At the time, a younger Sa'Raina Mahone, a junior HTC
Soldier, was accompanied by South Carolina's local
police. Shouting could be heard for miles. Xanpo and the
other fighters made a run for it, exiting through a hidden
tunnel to the east wing of the bar. Madin laid on the mat,
holding his bruised knee and trying to see where Jeffery
could have gone. There's no way he could've run away
that fast. The mystery champion was nowhere to be found.
Madin was surrounded with guns pointed in his direction.
Several audience members were detained, including the
commentator.

A few minutes later. Underground, standing and leaning on a wall in the sewers...

XANPO. *Sighs.* Hehehe. I can't believe I made it out. *Hears sewage water splashing and recognizes a voice as one of the fighters.*

DANTE. *Continues powerwalking fast, passing Xanpo.* Yo, man. I'd keep moving!!

SKY. *Following behind Dante, but keeps his eyes forward.* Up ahead there's a place the police won't catch us. Stay here and you're screwed.

He doesn't hesitate and follows the two warriors.

Twenty minutes later...

Miles away from the raided fight club bar and above ground, Xanpo and two other escaped fighters are resting. They're in an open field. Sky pulls out a digital map and pinpoints the nearest city is Neichest Town.

DANTE. Where'd you learn to fight?

XANPO. Hehe. You wouldn't believe me if I told you.

DANTE. Try me.

XANPO. Another world, soldier.

DANTE. *Confused.* Huh?

XANPO. Both of you fight like military recruits.

SKY. That we are. I'll be up for Staff Sergeant this November. Just taking a bit of leave time.

DANTE. *Nods at Xanpo.* Navy SEAL. A small training team, as of right now. Military living is hectic, bro. And dude!! Back there though. That big guy!

XANPO. I know right!! Too bad he was injured and couldn't getaway. *Shakes his head.*

SKY. He'll be fine. Madin doesn't have a criminal background.

DANTE. I didn't know you knew him.

SKY. We talked when we first arrived.

DANTE. *Chuckles.* There you go again, acting like a detective and shit.

SKY. *Laughs at the comment.* Maybe I'll be one. *He looks away.*

XANPO. *Intruding into the conversation.* You two are excellent fighters for Earth's standards.

DANTE. *Surprised and shocked.* Whoa, dude, like what the f–? Are you not human or something?

SKY. You look human…

XANPO. *Laughs.* I am. When I was younger, I was sent to another dimension by a weird machine in my science instructor's classroom.

SKY. The hell kind of an instructor was that?

XANPO. Heh. Beats me, bro.

DANTE. *Bewildered.* A – Another dimension, huh?

XANPO. *Ecstatic.* Bruh!! This dimension is quite similar, but the "humans" have powers. Some animals possess abilities too.

SKY. Okay, okay. *Snickers.* What are you smoking and where can we get some?

At this time, Sa'Raina surprises the group aiming a special gun-blaster at them. But, she lowers it.

SOLDIER SA'RAINA. Heh. Not from around these parts, huh? *Looking at Xanpo.*

XANPO. Um, no.

DANTE. What?! You going to shoot us or what?!! We have our rights! According to Law, we have the freedom to engage in fight clubs if we choose.

SKY. According to HighTech City Police Force, they have jurisdiction to arrest any person participates in illegal underground fight clubs around Georgia's vicinity to like 500 miles.

DANTE. Whose side are you on, brother?

SOLDIER SA'RAINA. Oh, save it. *Shakes her head.* You too military men I have no beef with. You serve our country… So do I. *Takes a few steps over to Xanpo.* You're not from around here. Why are you here?

XANPO. Why are you asking?

SOLDIER SA'RAINA. HTC Force has specific laws in place. Civilians who aren't residents must meet certain criteria before stepping anywhere near our city. So, don't make me ask you again.

DANTE. Fiesty! Hahahaa. Yeah!!! I like her.

SKY. He's –

SOLDIER SA'RAINA. *Doesn't look at Sky, maintains eye contact with Xanpo.* I didn't ask you.

XANPO. All right. *Hands up in a surrendering fashion for seconds and laughs.* Calm down. *Lowering his arms, he notices the time on his wristwatch.* But, I can't be too long. I'm supposed to be meeting up with a friend soon. If you follow me to Neichest, I'll explain more.

SOLDIER SA'RAINA. Let this be a trap.

XANPO. Worth your while. *Smiles and turns around to start walking.*

Time passes and the three warriors, plus the soldier, are at Mec's Family Bar & Tavern. This place changed a lot in terms of the present years in this story. Crystalia is sitting down at one of the round tables as the three men walk inside. Xanpo sees her sitting down, waves and gestures to Dante and Sky. They all sit and talk.

Something's off about his sorceress friend. She's not making eye contact. She's looking at the textile prints on the table cloth worriedly.

XANPO. *Concerned tone and speaks softly.* Crystalia. *Assumes based on her expressions.* You didn't sense any strange anomalies here in this world, did you?

CRYSTALIA. Not in this dimension, no. *Raises her head, looking up at Xanpo and nods. She turns to the three people sitting down at the table.* Who are they?

XANPO. Earth fighters.

CRYSTALIA. *A smile comes across her face.* They might be useful for what's happening.

XANPO. Well, that's a rather sudden change in attitude, so what're you talking about? What's happening?

CRYSTALIA. Quinoragoras are at it again. They've landed on planet Vrec. *Sighs worriedly.* King Oanayi's troops are defending the Damonarian Kingdom as we speak and the Prince is off-world seeking more assistance.

XANPO. He'll be having more trouble looking for our Xeiar friends. *Shakes his head and sighs.*

CRYSTALIA. Not to mention their planet was automatically placed on lockdown; there's no easy entrance if you aren't of magical blood.

XANPO. *He then lowers his head and stares at the table.* We can't do this here. *Turns to look at his new friends then looks straight ahead at the sorceress.* Let's find a secure place to talk.

The group leaves the bar and heads down to the Techy Mountains. Upon leaving the place, they go behind the building and the sorceress teleports them to the mountains at Sky's mention. Arriving at the vacant mountains, Crystalia whipped her crystal ball out of thin air. Sky, Dante, and Sa'Raina asked to assist, in any shape or form, even though they'll be at a disadvantage. They knew the risks and felt it as a challenge to improve themselves mentally and physically.

A small creature, living inside Crystalia's ball, decided to vibrate multiple times, insinuating a trans-dimensional call was coming through from a faraway distance. Two of Xanpo's Xeiar friends, Jorgo and Isanto, were coming to Earth to take them all to the fight in Namorant.

MEANWHILE, ON PLANET VREC...

An hour before to contacting Crystalia on Earth, Jorgo and Isanto, on planet Xeiar, in the Namorant Dimension, stopped by Grand Xesus and asked what the Great Wizards were going to do about this situation. They left them in the dark but told the two wizards to gather as many local warrior wizards to help out. After the two wizards left their presence, the Great Xeiars discussed another plan. They agreed to move their planet to another dimension. Of course, this did not happen because it would require excessive amounts of Xeiar magic needed to perform such a spell. It would obliterate any sole wizard, no matter how strong the wizard. So, Xeiar was moved far off on its own and away from the other planets.

Jorgo and Isanto teleported to Earth, with the help of a transport relic. They brought Xanpo, Crystalia, Dante, Sa'Raina, and Sky to planet Vrec to assist in the fight. Unfortunately, a trans-dimensional push happened and a few heroes went to different places on planet Vrec.

Arriving at the Namorant Dimension, miles away from the kingdom.

From the look of things, the Quinoragoras have been on planet Vrec since before the heroes all knew of this invasion attack. King Gorvin, leader of the Quinoragoras, gave the command to annihilate this planet and enter King Oanayi's gates.

The all-powerful evil King led an army of Quinoragoras through planet Vrec, but could not find the place. Xeiar wizards were there to cause distractions and magically transport all of the creatures to a desolate area on the planet... far away from the Damonarian Kingdom.

The group only found three of Gorvin's top generals. A fiery one, a wintery one, and a dark mole variant of the demonic alien race.

DAMONARIAN V. QUINORAGORAS WAR! – PLANET VREC.

The crackling chill in the air was almost enough to counteract the flames in the Generals' hearts. Almost.

XANPO. Gentleman, it seems we've reached the point of conflict that can only be dispelled by... *He cracks his knuckles.* Physical means.

GALACIEON. We have no problem with that, do we?

REDILEON. No problem with killing you useless curs. *Chuckles.* I am still quite ravenous for Damonarian blood. *Licks his lips with his long lizard-like tongue.*

The Generals stand in a line, baring their claws and begin baring their teeth which resemble a shark's jaw. Snarling reverberates from the three Quinoragoras Generals, but it does little to phase their opposing forces.

ARIES. *He looks at his fighters and smirks. He turns back to look at the creatures as his right-hand sparks.* This should be more comfortable.

The wizard does a clothing-change spell on the human heroes; including Xanpo, allowing their gear and weapons (to which they naturally use) to appear on their person.

XANPO. Much appreciated, Aries.

ARIES. You're welcome, brother.

ZANARI. *Shouts to his comrades.* Formation T!!

A chorus of chants in response fights back in the verbal war, and the four warriors form a pentagon.

The forces charged towards each other, colliding in hand-to-hand combat. Jorgo, Zanari, and Aries reached the fight first.

Jorgo ducked down narrowly missing Galacieon's hateful blow, before turning back to set his enemy back with a spinning kick. Balancing low, Jorgo smirks as Galacieon crumples. However, the kick only serves to anger him further.

Isanto mutters a spell and draws out a bow and arrow. He taunts against the string and aims for Redileon. Two arrows whistle past, screaming past his target's ear. Isanto cries in frustration as the fiery creature, like a wild bull, continues to charge forward.

ISANTO. *Whispering.* Damn it.

JORGO. *Shouting.* This isn't working. They're too fast!

ZANARI. *His eyes look to Jorgo.* Then we have to be faster, don't we?! *Looking back at the creatures.* Now!!

The ice crunches as Aries charges forward, his fists clenched and ready. He swings downwards with one hand aiming for the nose, whilst elbowing to aim for the throat. Virlores manages to dodge the first blow, but grunts in pain as his throat is punched.

Aries tries to grab Virlores' neck but is tackled instead. Virlores is on top of him, punching him in the face nonstop. He's thrown off after a few seconds, rolling, and crashing against a dying tree.

VIRLORES. *Rageful shouting.* You insolent–

ARIES. I'll have you know, you're the one who's truly disgusting here. Killing innocents, wreaking havoc everywhere you go! We'll stop this war before any more planets are annihilated!!

VIRLORES. Hehee. You may try. *Sneers.* So… Where have you been to stop us, eh Wizard? Your kind may be potential Gods to other inferior creatures, but you all are– *Voice raises!* –cowards!!! The lot of you!

In his rage the creature flung himself forward, punching Aries in the ribs. He ran his nails harshly down the warrior's face, etching a large scar on his face.

XANPO. *Shouting from a short distance where he's fighting.* Why the hell are you two playing?! Beat the scum!!

He drew his iron ax, slowly crouching and walking to Redileon, where Isanto has his magical light-based bow string wrapped around Redileon's neck. The string is taunt, choking him while Xanpo raises his ax, swinging for the heart.

Redileon moves to face Isanto quickly, dodging the swing of the weapon and snapping the bowstring. The magical light-based bow turns into tiny particles and disappear.

Isanto furiously rains a flurry of punches on Redileon, going for his arms, punching every muscle. Redileon, dazed, shakes his injured arms before pushing forward, lashing out in uncontrolled rage. He faces both men as they throw punches. All Redileon can do is block them with his hands, until Xanpo strikes his stomach.

Xanpo grunts as he sinks the sharp tip deeper and Redileon grows silent. The creature falls to his knees, chuckling in pain as he closes his eyes peacefully. Xanpo pushes forward until the tip comes out to the other side, killing the fiery Quinoragoras creature.

XANPO. You finally die, creature.

ISANTO. About time too.

Galacieon and Virlores turn to see their fallen brother, and growl in pitted rage when they see his corpse kneeling on the ground... not yet have fallen.

The icy creature dodges Zanari's kick to the leg, and catches it instead, turning it until a loud snap is heard. Zanari yells in pain, faltering as Galacieon punches his knee.

ZANARI. AAAAAAHHHHHH!!!! You son-of-a-BITCH!!!! Aaaahhhh!!

ISANTO. *Grits his teeth.* Argh... You damn monster!

Isanto and Xanpo charge towards Galacieon. Xanpo reaches for his iron ax lying on the ground then swings to cleave Galacieon's head, but he ducks and head-butts Xanpo.

JORGO. *Shouts across the battlefield.* Aries, get over here!! I
   need back up!

Aries runs in wide strides, attacking Virlores from behind.
Jorgo and Aries try to tackle and trap the creature in a bind,
but hold after hold and blow after blow, Virlores evades
them. The creature throws back his head and sends black-
colored sharp vines erupting from his body, spearing Aries
and Jorgo through the leg and chest.

Virlores runs to the top of a mountain, growling at the
harsh wind as he does so. Aries falls back, unable to run,
clutching his leg in pain. Jorgo clutches his chest, panting
on the ground.

ARIES. It's not working!! *His internal Xeiar healing ability fixes
   his leg.* We can't let him enter civilian territory!

Jorgo stays silent for a moment, after looking at Isanto's
magical arrows flying towards Galacieon.

JORGO. *Thinking of a plan.* Aries, shield!!

The warrior nods and grabs the heavy wood, grunting as
he lifts it on his shoulder. Jorgo stands up, running towards
the shield and jumps on it, propelling himself into the air to
the top of the dirt-made stairs where Virlores is currently.

An animal-like growl rips through the air as Jorgo attacks
Virlores, trapping him against the wall and punching his
face, repeatedly. Jorgo swings the chain he pulled out of his
sash. Virlores ducks twice, backing away. But he is struck on

the third swing, and the chains quickly trap him, binding him tightly.

ARIES. Jorgo! *Mutters a spell and produces a materialized wooden weapon.* Spear!! *Throws it.*

The spear sails through the air, striking Virlores.

Jorgo drops Virlores off the cliff – unseen by the audience.

At this time the Prince's leg is healed, but now he's in an intense fight with the icy creature. Galacieon is seen biting Zanari in the neck, seemingly killing him before the other warriors come to his aid. His eyes turned completely white.

ISANTO. NO!!!! Zanari!!

XANPO. *Yells.* You will die for that!

The two warriors gain up on Galacieon, surrounding him with a bow and an ax. Like two trainers to a lion, they wait to attack, crouched low.

Slowly, they corner Galacieon, not flinching when he snarls and bites at them. Xanpo makes his move first, striking with his iron ax, while Isanto shoots from the other side. Galacieon narrowly misses the ax blow, but the magical light-based arrow hits him square in the chest.

He stops for a moment, and Xanpo swings again. Isanto distracts Galacieon by swinging at his left side before Xanpo slices the creature's middle. Isanto shoots again, and Galacieon staggers with two arrows in his chest.

ISANTO. Die… *Breathes out slow.* You beast.

Galacieon slowly sinks, collapsing and dying on his knees in front of the warriors.

The sands reverberated with the isolated battle of three warriors against three foul beasts. The Quinoragoras were angrier than ever, having been disturbed from their meal. The two wizards had resorted to throwing close combat spells, making the monsters disorientated, before spearing them multiple times.

Their skin seemed hardened by rage, and their cries shrill as the wind swept around them.

Slowly, the three warriors were able to gang up on the last snarling creature, before bringing it down from all three angles.

The warriors' chests heaved as they stood in front of their handiwork.

Isanto, Xanpo, and Jorgo check to see if Zanari is still alive. To their dismay, there's a small faction to his breathing, but for in his eyes… It looks like he is lost. Isanto does a quick healing spell to stop the Prince from moving closer to Death's Door.

JORGO. They'll send more. We're just lucky King Gorvin isn't here.

XANPO. Probably on another world with the lower Quinoragoras spawn. *Tightens his right fist and grits his teeth*. Damn. I wish this supposedly great almighty King was here! He'll pay for what his Generals have done to Zanari!

ISANTO. Be careful what you wish for Xanpo. *His eyes leer to his little brother.*

Aries joins them, looking fully rejuvenated and ready for another battle.

ARIES. If the King indeed does bring more of the Quinoragoras, we'll end them all! Right here!!

XANPO. *Remembering people he traveled to Namorant with before being split up due to the transport spell.* There are other warriors… Sa'Raina, Sky, and Dante should be arriving soon. *Remembering another.* And Cryst!

ZANARI. *Weakly, but recovering.* He – should be here soon.

Just then crying is heard in the distance. Aries goes to check it out. The huge boulders fifty yards out from their present location. He returns with a child in his arms. She is quivering in fear, but unharmed.

ISANTO. Brother! Was the child alone?

XANPO. Were there bodies surrounding her?

ARIES. No. Not a soul in sight. I mean, unless they were obliterated awhile before we came to this area and stopped the three Generals.

ISANTO. *Sighs.* Take her to the closest but safest village where Quinoragoras haven't wrecked yet and tell them to evacuate.

JORGO. …Immediately!! *He adds on, feeling hatred burning inside him and thinking about his infant daughters' possible fate.*

ISANTO. I think a larger, more ferocious wolf is needed to recharge our ranks. *Sighs.* Cryst isn't going to be happy when he learns what they did to the Prince.

XANPO. *Looks directly at Aries.* You must send word to the others in case more come. Get the other warriors! Anyone that can join us.

Isanto nods to Aries, who materializes hawk-fairy wings. They open up majestically. Red as blood and simmering gold. He takes off, flying elsewhere to look for the reinforcements, and Cryst, whom half were relocated thanks to the Trans-dimensional Push which was affected by a faulty transport relic Jorgo and Isanto used.

XANPO. So what do you suggest now? We just sit here and wait?

JORGO. There is nothing we can do. Let's hope there are members of the first rank that can be spared from planet Coroth and Vaoth to help us. We need to give the surviving villagers here some time to evacuate.

XANPO. I don't think Drekye and Kokashi should leave their world. They're the strongest few on Coroth.

JORGO. Figures. *Shakes his head.* The other two are always busy so we most likely couldn't find those guys anyway... What about the Huntress female, Quarah?

XANPO. I heard she's off-world at the moment dealing with ghostly Penialia creatures.

On planet Extiepenia, there are homo-sapien humans whose powers derive from supernatural and paranormal forces. The inhabitants of this world resemble Earth human beings, but their eyes are different. Each Extiepian individual is completely different. Staring into one of their eyes, you'll notice the difference. They're alien. Deep underground lives powerful ghost creatures, Penialia's. They sleep a lot, but during seasonal cycles and births, they awaken. Their primal purpose is to seek an Extiepian and make them their host body. Penialia's are transparent creatures. Their bodies are ghostly. The young ghostly creatures typically merge with an adolescence Extiepian child.

ISANTO. I think we need to regroup. We need formation. If we join the others, we can't just mindlessly kill as we did before against those three Quinoragoras.

JORGO. *Having just muttered a spell and materializes his unique and powerful blade, he thinks about the Quinoragoras King.* I think when the King arrives, we should leave the talking to me.

XANPO. Bruh! *Shakes his head.* Always brute force with you, huh?! I expect this from Isanto mainly because of his size. Haven't you learned anything, Jorgo? People are killed with words, in fact, the worst enemies do the most talking. That's insanely accurate!!

ISANTO. Haha. Funny, Xanpo. *Shakes his head with a smile.*

XANPO. Well, the Quinoragoras are dumb animals. Deadly when they get to you, but before that, very possible to take out.

ISANTO. Jorgo… Did you make sure your wife and daughter made it off Xeiar?

JORGO. Heh. *Shakes his head.* My wife's stubborn ass. *Laughs.* We ended up asking my mother – hours before this war even started. *Smiles with his eyes closed for seconds.* Before we brought you all here, myself and Isanto went to Grand Xesus. I tried to talk them into helping, but they ignored us. Pfft… *Annoyed sigh.* My mother agreed to take my daughter to another world. I don't know where though. But hey! I'm surprised you let your baby brother fight with us this time.

XANPO. Yeeeeaaaahhhh. I agree. I assumed you figured we needed his unique Xeiar skills.

ISANTO. Pfft. I got tired of him begging. Plus our mother insisted.

The Human-Damonarian cross-breed, Xanpo, starts feeling pains arising in his muscles. The others are looking rather exhausted to engage in another battle as well.

XANPO. We should get the medkit.

JORGO. Good thinking.

Xanpo walks to a battered case which opens squeakily and starts bandaging his little to no bleeding arm, wrapping it around and up to his forearms.

The three remaining warriors make up a new plan in a corner of the desolate landscape.

As time passes, the sands grow weary and circulate them.

Each grain of sand is a grey-silver, shining in the moonlight. The dunes gathered in the night, each gust of wind that blew took the shimmering grains on a new journey.

This was the unnamed, lost desert on Vrec where one would describe its landscape as barren, yet beautiful. Not even the blood from those who died here could stop the sands from moving, reforming new dunes to hide the death and destruction that ensued.

The battlefield where they fought and killed the three Quinoragoras generals only consisted of four black remnants of wall left behind by the last battle. The remnants were of an old castle, with only a long chain as evidence of a drawbridge.

What feels like hours, only forty (Earth) minutes have passed…

The warriors got in a brief time of relaxation, to relieve their tired muscles. Aries returns with three humans… Dante, Sa'Raina, Sky, and Cryst.

ARIES. Any signs of them since I left?

ISANTO. No, but when they do come, we'll be ready.

CRYST. Less talk, more avenging. *Cracks his knuckles.*

DANTE. Are we really on a mission to end this King Gorvin? That's easier said than done from what I've heard.

ZANARI. We'll do… The Crane Formation. I'm sure you three Earthlings know it, right?

XANPO. They're quick to learn. *Laughs.*

ZANARI. Well, it's our best chance against mindless beasts.

SA'RAINA. The Crane Formation it is. I like it! Sounds… Old school.

SKY. Ending that king will be a bonus to the people in the Namorant Dimension.

SA'RAINA. *Sighs joyfully.* I'm sure once he sees what we can do as a cohesive unit, he'll hide like the coward he truly is.

XANPO. *Hearing his friends' over-confidence.* Heh. That doesn't sound like you, Sa'Raina. Over-analyzing an opponent especially one you've never done battle with before can cause major implications that'll make it hard to recover.

Suddenly the sands swirled around them – all looked towards Aries' large magical wings, but he just shrugged.

CRYST. *Tenses up.* This is it!! *Tightens his fists and exhales calmly.*

He shifted into his beast form, becoming three times his size. The Damonarian beast, slightly resembling an Earth's werewolf, snarled in anticipation.

King Gorvin appeared in fiery light, holding a Transporter Relic in his left hand, and staff, of what appears to be made of some kind of alien metal, in the other.

JORGO. Greetings King Gorvin. I am Jorgo–

GORVIN. Heh-heh. No need for formalities. I know who you all are. You killed three of my faithful Generals. *Exhales while glancing down at their corpses for seconds.* No pity. *Growls.* Though it seems as if they nearly got one of yours too. Pity they didn't kill you all.

ZANARI. Oh… I am all healed up now. What're you waiting for, my king? If you're here for a fight, then surely you shall not be disappointed by your impending demise.

GORVIN. Well… You all seem particularly confident. I might as well let out my true army!

The Transporter Relic activates in Gorvin's right hand and suddenly from behind him, other Quinoragoras creatures stream onto the desert sands in large groups.

GORVIN. Enjoy more of my kind, you otherworld warriors…

The Xeiar Wizards erected their shields as the other fighters got into two lines inside a circle.

Isanto and Jorgo formed the first line, while Xanpo and Dante made the second line with their weapons. Sa'Raina and Sky formed the left side, holding their swords up. Cryst made the left side, barely being held back by Aries' instructions.

No longer wounded and stumbling, but fully healed, Zanari gets beside Cryst.

GORVIN. Haha. That one may be closer to death. *He laughs derisively at Zanari's recovering stance.*

Xanpo is shaking his head, knowing full well Zanari's nature but glad he's joining his brother's in a battle against their enemies to end this war once and for all.

XANPO. *Paying attention to King Gorvin and speaks out loud.* Glad you're with us, Zanari.

JORGO. Same here! *He smiles for a brief second.*

ISANTO. Ready, brother? *Speaking directly to Aries.*

ARIES. You bet. Let's get this battle started.

Aries takes off, his magical large grey wings beating strongly leaving behind sparkles of light-residue behind.

He chants inside his mind about his sole job to reduce the masses of Quinoragoras, whilst leading the formations.

The foul beasts are running into the shields which were charmed to let things out, such as the arrows from Isanto, but keep all else out. Aries continues to fly around, pushing the beasts back past the walls to the old castle. However, they still keep coming.

ARIES. *He yells out.* T!! *Smiling as the shield drops and their enemy comes swarming in.*

The first assault involved the warriors with weapons, and hand-to-hand combat forms the first line.

The two wizards, Jorgo and Isanto, continue to shoot arrows from the backline... Jorgo following Isanto's spells. Despite their differences, they had a certain gleam in their eyes as they hit every one of their marks.

"U!" Xanpo called out, just before the line broke down the middle and the runners made their way towards a semi-circle. The front line split apart, and blindly, the beasts ran straight into large spears held by the second line of warriors. Whilst the second line switched to close combat. The first line closed off and set the shield again, trapping a large group of Quinoragoras.

Sa'Raina and Sky took over with tripwires that sliced the Quinoragoras' legs. Slowly, they pile up, as they can no longer charge.

Aries swoops down to throw the dying beasts elsewhere before their bodies accumulated to form a wall – a wall that they could easily jump and attack from a higher point.

After a while, the beasts came up the sides of the shield even though the warrior's method was working. Soon they were overwhelmed – and the shield wouldn't hold forever.

"R!" Isanto called out, swooping down to clear the swelling ranks that charged on the sides.

The semi-circle opened again with two lines that fanned out from the circle, fighting the enemy in a V shape.

An unseen female warrior with a green coloring as part of her human skin pigment, sixteen-year-old Princess Chloe, discreetly and unnoticed is on top of a castle wall and continues fighting with her extensive planet Vaoth martial arts training, while Xanpo joined Isanto and Jorgo in the V formation. Each pair were back-to-back, fighting the snapping beasts as best they could.

Aries tries to give them time to recover, but the King simply summoned the whole lot of them. More and more of them, no matter how many dead beasts laid on the floor.

"T!" Aries ordered from above, swooping down to get the Quinoragoras in line.

Warriors form a laneway, and Cryst runs down, throwing the beasts into the air while Jorgo and Isanto shoot them. It was almost a comical sight as the beasts were chucked upwards, touching the sky, only to fall back down, dead. More than a few times, the warriors had to dodge the falling corpses.

"L!" Xanpo called out, joining his fellow warriors. Now they just had to keep the beasts at bay. But before, he descended, out of the corner of his eye, he saw Sky on the back of a female Quinoragoras, wrestling the creature to the ground by tightening his chokehold more and more.

This monster had a special coat on, indicating status. Before anyone could get to him, thinking he needs assistance, the sharp, ruthless teeth ripped into Sky's left forearm and leaving him bleeding out in a pool of his blood.

Sa'Raina emerges from the dark greyed out bushes (mostly twigs sticking out the greyed sands), using a special blaster and shooting a pathway through the beasts. She is unnoticed, for the time being, sneaking through the battlefield and sees the female Quinoragoras. She unleashes a barrage of laser blasts at the creatures while running to her. Sa'Raina reaches her target, firing comes to a halt, jumps in the air, and knees the female Quinoragoras to the ground. She finishes off the creature by stomping down on her chest ruthlessly and blasting her in the face ending the creature's life.

XANPO. NO! Sky! *He finishes off a Quinoragoras by half turning into a Damonarian beast for a second. He changes back, making his way to his friend. He left his post, ignoring Isanto's orders.* Sky! Please don't leave us!! *He places his hands over Sky's wounds, assisting in potentially stopping the bleeding.* You can't, we need you by our side. Remember the deal after the fight club? I fight, you fight. I die, you die. Please, listen to me… Sky?

SKY. God, Xanpo! You see I'm wounded, but I'm not out just yet. And the Hell… *Chuckles weakly…* I have never said those words to you.

KING GORVIN. Heh. *He cuts in.* He's right assuming your human body can't hold off against Quinoragoras's bite. Hahaha hahaha.

While fighting a few Quinoragoras on his own and behind Gorvin, Isanto shoots a spell at the king.

All he could do was blink, not realizing Sky and the other humans volunteered their lives for the future of the Namorant Dimension's safety. Xanpo lets go of Sky's wound after applying a makeshift bandage.

XANPO. All right! If you die, I'll come to Darkeil and kick your ass. *Laughs jokingly.*

The battle rages on… Xanpo speeds off and helps to defeat as many Quinoragoras as he can.

ARIES. *Using his peripheral vision to view Sky.* Eh… I'm deeply
      sorry. Looks like you're out. *Whispers a safe house spell
      for Sky to recover in while pushing back three creatures.*

Jorgo and the rest of the warriors start moving closer to Sky's
safe housing and help maintain a Quinoragoras-free zone,
ensuring that he has enough time to recover.

The warriors form a square shape, determined to kill the
remaining Quinoragoras.

Aries could see the King was getting irritatingly annoyed,
as the creatures slowed down, and soon noticing how his
species weren't coming out of the portal anymore.

Isanto's little brother tried to go after the King but is stopped
by an icy Quinoragoras. His magical light-based wings
batting him down to the ground.

ARIES. You aren't going anywhere!

GORVIN. You've proven you and your warriors are quite
      the murderers. Too bad for the human.

ARIES. You will pay for what your mutts did to him.

GORVIN. I am looking for warriors such as yourselves
      to join my kingdom. You could be great! I'm sure
      you're tired of fighting endless battles.

ARIES. We would never fight for you. *Walked towards the
      King's body as he outwardly shook.*

The rage seemed to pour off him in waves, but the King stood strongly, prepared to fight. Xanpo joined Aries and the three jumped into fierce combat.

The King towered over both of them but swung slowly from above. His left hand held a large chain and mace. Aries flew slightly off the ground, trying to get higher opportunities, but he could only dodge the mace that swung towards his head.

Xanpo attacked whenever the King's attention was on Aries, but the King's skin could not be pierced.

In blind fury, Xanpo punched the King's neck, smirking as he stumbled back. The King stalked towards him and aimed to punch him in the stomach, but was blocked by Aries' wings, whilst Dante leaped up and elbowed him in the head.

GORVIN. *Stumbled, angrier than ever. He looked at the relic on his body and smiled a bloody smile.* I am not sorry to have to do this.

Giant wings closed around him as the King held the relic towards his chest, shooting a large beam towards Aries.

Aries screamed, shooting back all the power he could give. His wings were only a defense mechanism, but for a moment it seemed like the battle was frozen. Panting from all the power that surged towards him, Aries grimaced as he felt something build in his chest. He couldn't keep this up forever.

ARIES. Isanto, Jorgo I… I can't do this. You have to help me!!!!

It was an endless play between powers as the king's spell came closer and closer to piercing his wings.

Isanto ran towards Aries with an orange-colored ball of energy building in his hands but failed to notice the general Quinoragoras' form hiding in the bushes.

The general leaped out, taking Isanto by surprise. He was forced to the ground as the general lashed out at him, snapping and snarling.

JORGO. No! Isanto!

He ran up to the pair, trying to pierce the general's chest with his dagger. Dante joined him, jumping from the wall above and sticking a dagger in his back, but was soon thrown off.

Aries groaned at the losing battle. It was all too soon before Aries was bitten from his side, crushing his rib cage.

ISANTO. No... No, brother!!!!

The king smiled and pushed even further as Aries weakened.

Tears of rage ran down his eyes, even when Xanpo and Sa'Raina came to help him. Cryst ran towards the general and finally brought the beast down alongside Jorgo, whose spells weakened the monster's attacks.

Before the warriors could break the spell, something happened. The ground started shaking, and everything melted away, except the light in Aries' chest. He cried as he let out the light no longer contained. Sky and Isanto were exhausted.

Aries' body shook as he let go, and Gorvin's spell seemed to slash into his body. Aries' eyes turned a pale blue and his wings carried him slightly off the ground. The battle had halted as people became blinded by the light.

The mighty King Gorvin stood proudly with a smirk on his rugged face.

GORVIN. So, you have chosen a most barbarous death. *Sneers remorselessly.* I see... Heh-heh. I shall enjoy killing the lot of you even more.

XANPO. *Points in the King's direction and speaks with passion.* Not if we kill you first!

The warrior spoke more confidently passionate than he felt at the start.

Warriors stood beside him, yet the air thickened with caution as Gorvin's claws slowly unsheathed. A few seconds pass and he started opening his hands wide. Despite what he felt on the inside, Xanpo couldn't hide his gulp at the knife-like claws glistened.

Five seconds went by...

The warriors exchanged sideways glances, nodding quickly at one another.

ISANTO. *Taking charge, voice loud and strong.* Warriors... Now!!

With a barbaric but ghastly growl, King Gorvin and his Quinoragoras group of followers leap into battle.

All seven remaining warriors, not the incognito one, run in all directions, towards the vicious creatures. The group of warriors consisting of three Damonarian warriors, two humans, and two Xeiar wizards. They charge forward, trying to surround the large, monstrous leader.

Sa'Raina and Isanto are on the left, getting to higher ground and they start shooting approximately twenty Quinoragoras that have charged at them.

Isanto shoots three magical light-based arrows, aiming directly for a blow to the eye, but the King avoids the first two and catches the last arrow mid-flight.

The warriors, all in shock, stop running in their formation and stare at the arrow just centimeters from the King's face. His voice turns to a thunderous yell as he begins to double in size, like an erupting volcano.

Xanpo, Cryst, and Zanari took the right flank, while Jorgo and Dante took the front and back.

The three Damonarians – the strongest, yet only two are the calmest in the group – shift into their beast forms, are yowling with the pain to their transformation. Their voices turn into monstrous growls as they begin to double in size, stretching out their bodies as the torso becomes long and lean. One Damonarian yelped as his teeth grew, baring themselves in all their glory. Fur began to erupt from their backs while their legs forced them to stand on all fours.

In mere minutes, two grey-haired, and one brown-haired, beast stood before Jorgo, a half-recovered Sky, and Dante. The three transformed warriors are ready to strike.

On higher ground, Isanto is firing magical arrows at some of the creatures, Sa'Raina firing her blaster, and very few are easily dodging the attacks pointing in their direction. One of their fellow Quinoragoras brethren weren't so lucky. Sa'Raina slipped past, smirked at the angry creatures who saw the destruction of their brother-in-arms even as she kept going. Each time she hit her target, more and more Quinoragoras creatures were closing in on her.

The warriors continued using their desired weapons to at least wound the giant, but to no avail are they successful.

Sky, Jorgo, and Dante take the right flank, fighting their way through a gang of fifty. The King stood, surrounded by a ring of his followers, taking in the scene with thunderous and booming laughter. His claws were still out, but he would not join the fight again just yet.

JORGO. *Shouting from a distance, far from the wizard Isanto.* Down!!

The wizard places his hands in a triangle shape towards the sky, making the clouds swirl and become grey and heavy. After a few moments, he directs lightning strikes to the remaining Quinoragoras, frying them where they stand and two larger ones strike the King's torso.

The demonic-looking creature's growl in unison before continuing the battle, this time, with a large target upon Jorgo. The King is furious. He takes a second to recover.

Cryst attacks from behind, half- transformed and using his claws to scratch the legs of the enemy. While he causes some large wounds, the King quickly turns around and grabs him by the neck. The warrior chokes, claws scratching at the King's hand that is slowly closing around his windpipe.

ISANTO. *Voice loud and strong.* Fall-back!!!! We need to regroup!

Isanto orders, not noticing a young girl continuing to fight on the sidelines.

Chloe, an odd-looking young teen warrior is near a cave-like rock face, throwing knives towards the King's back. She uses ten knives before landing one to his left shoulder. This makes him roar and turns back, dropping Cryst and giving the seven warriors a chance to regroup.

The teen girl, with a color as close to lime-green for hair color and a lighter variation of the same color to her human skin pigment, smiles from the cave when she realizes the King cannot see her and slinks back into darkness.

Two (Earth) minutes pass...

The seven warriors escape to another hiding, whilst Dante and Sky make a quick barricade of large fallen branches. They shoot at the gathering army, utilizing their human-made advanced laser blasters, looking worriedly at each other.

After a constant barrage of assaults, they realize their weaponry isn't phasing him as his expression is unfazed.

ISANTO. Well, I'm done. Anyone else got any bright ideas? Cuz' none of our weapons and attacks affect him. *Almost doubting himself.* There's too many of them! At this rate, we'll never get to the King!

CRYST. *Shaking his head a few times.* Damonarians and the All-Powerful Xeiars seem to be doing nothing to him. *Speaking to no one in particular.* Has his body been experimented on, making it impenetrable to our attacks?

XANPO. *Eyes watching Gorvin at the moment.* I don't know. Our only chance is if we create a diversion. *Turns to look at his comrades.* Draw the King to the dark river to the east.

JORGO. These rivers aren't like on Earth, Xanpo. You know that!! The river is precarious, and the water won't give us much of an advant– Ah!!!! *Shielding himself from debris.*

ZANARI. Some advantage is better than nothing. *Turns to look at Sa'Raina.* Stay with Cryst. The rest of us will redirect to the river.

SA'RAINA. Good luck. We'll regroup later. We need to band together and knock off some of the protection around the King.

JORGO. Alright. The rest of you on me.

The Xeiar Wizard, Jorgo, takes charge for a while and stands at the top of the rock. He places his balled-up fist in front of his mouth, murmurs a spell and speaks into his fist. He's exhaling – blowing – at a pitch that grabs the attention of the Quinoragoras creatures. Now they have all changed and are continuing to swarm the three warriors.

The rest of the warrior's nod before following the sound of Jorgo's low-pitched horn.

The King grunts in frustration, muttering something about the low wits of "fleshlings", before making his way to the river.

GORVIN. Let's see what you do against old foes.

The King places his hands upon the dirt muttering a spell, while the warriors are fighting against his followers. The wizards hear the enchantment with confusing stares on their faces.

JORGO. *Shouts with his eyes on Gorvin and fighting off two Quinoragoras.* Okay! What traitorous Xeiar taught him that?!

Two medium average-sized, grey-haired creatures attacked the trio. They are snarling and biting as they attempt to leap over the large rock all three were standing on.

A brown haired, slim and skinny Quinoragoras slowly stalked the side of the rock, licking his lips as he stared at his next target.

SA'RAINA. *Turns her head abruptly to her right and shouts.* Look out, Cryst!!!!

The brown-haired creature lunged forward before Sa'Raina had a chance to throw her weapon, jumping higher than any other Quinoragoras.

JORGO. *Hearing faint, sneaking noises and turns around.* No!!!!!!!!

Sa'Raina and Cryst are knocked to the ground. The Damonarian warrior is then bitten in the neck. Blood gushes out of him and Sa'Raina and Jorgo exchange lost looks of defeat. Cryst's neck had been gouged out by a murderous, bloodthirsty and barbaric Quinoragoras. He's reverted to his human-like form, staring straight at the dark blue maroon sky, lying on the ground lifeless.

Jorgo rushes over to Cryst's body and drags his cold body to the back of the huge boulder-like rock. Isanto, having teleported near the body just now, covers him and continues to fire magical energy spell-blasts at the enemies.

Meanwhile, somewhere very close to the others and completely concealed from the group, Chloe is continuously fighting some Quinoragoras with her bare hands, leaping on one of their backs and strangling it 'til it can't fight anymore. The creature attempts to buck her off, but to no avail.

The King reaches the river and he strode right in, crossing it with great splashes. He created his waves, scowling at the remaining warriors.

By the murky river, Sky is fighting alongside Dante, their swords slice through the foul monsters that have sloshed across the river. Suddenly, one creature attacks from behind where Aries is lying unconscious.

SKY. *Calling for reinforcements.* Xanpo!! *Pushes a creature back.*
Get off you mongrel!

Sky continues to swing his heavy sword but doesn't stab them quick enough to get to Xanpo. Using one hand is tricky, but he's pulling it off with skill and style.

A tacky shield lies next to him as he is pushed on his back. Large teeth bare towards his head, he immediately goes for the shield to protect his life.

The creature continues to snarl, before giving up, and rising to its hind legs, taking Sky by surprise. His weakened and not fully healed yet arm cannot help to hold the shield, leaving him exposed.

ZANARI. No! *Growls.* Sky! *Fighting off three creatures at once.*

Sky attempts to stand, but he gets knocked to the ground again, along with Zanari, by one of the waves, causing Jorgo to quickly conjure up the waters, swirling them in his palm. He's not verballing doing anything.

Meanwhile, Isanto has leaped on the King's back and started to strangle him. He attempts to buck the wizard off but to no avail because of his tight hold on him.

By the river, Sky is fighting alongside Jorgo, their huge sharp knives slice through the side of the King where his skin-armor has been sliced off. Jorgo swoops in unnoticed and manages to land a few blows, but the King retaliates by using his claws to scratch his entire body.

Another creature comes down with a large crunch, landing upon Sky's chest, nearly breaking his ribs. His lungs fill with blood and he chokes just as Jorgo gets to him.

Some of Sky's blood flows to the water's edge, painting the river scarlet red.

JORGO. NOOOOOO!!!!! **Bargo Excamei!!** *He shouted as all Quinoragoras was suddenly pushed aside.* Come on Sky! *He falls near Sky's body. He can hear his faint breathing.* Stay with us. *Clutching onto his wound and attempting to compress it.* Come on! *He closes his eyes just briefly and exhales for four seconds.* **Healoris.**

Sky's eyes close and his bleeding slows. Jorgo removes his hands from Sky's wounds.

XANPO. *Rushes closer to Jorgo and Sky, gnarling as he's trashing through a dozen Quinoragoras. He saw Jorgo close his eyes during battle.* Never close your eyes during a battle!!!!

JORGO. *Not focusing on anything else but the king at the moment.* Damn YOU! *He gets to his feet, staring at Gorvin. Eyes squaring down on his next target.*

The wizard drags Sky's body to a safe place, then he glances up and sees Dante has fallen as well. Sa'Raina is with him.

SA'RAINA. Come on, Dante. *She sobs.* I got you, buddy.

Jorgo starts to swirl the waters again while yelling for Isanto to save Sky, cornered next to an unconscious Aries. His shield lies next to him as he is on his back, his hands the only barrier between the large claws and his head.

The King shows no mercy and lifts his hand quickly, before piercing a long nail into Aries's chest. His lungs fill with blood and he chokes just as Isanto gets to him.

ISANTO. Nearly reaching him. NO! Brotherrrrrr!!!!

Zanari continues to push the King back with extra force, grief sinking into his chest making his powers a lot stronger, yet uncontrollable. His inner beast is about to consume him.

ISANTO. Come on, Aries. Little brother, don't give up just yet! Stay with us. Come on! *He's holding his brother, constantly shaking his bruised body.*

ARIES. *In a final breath, he breathes out.* Sorry… Br – *His whole body becomes limp in Isanto's arms.*

ISANTO. No… *Shaking his head disbelievingly.* No… it can't be.

Aries's blood flows to the water's edge, painting the river red. His eyes lose color as they become soulless.

Isanto, still with a look of disbelief upon his face, clutches onto Aries's hands and compressing his wound.

XANPO. *Shakes his head.* Damn it. *He whispered.*

Jorgo appears by Isanto and pulls his arms, helping him let go and they drag Aries's lifeless body to a safe place.

JORGO. We'll kick his ass. This one's not leaving here alive. We'll finish this, Isanto.

A minute passes and Gorvin sits patiently with a smirk on his face, allowing the warriors to grieve.

Dante glances at the creature and sees his scandalous expression. He turns to Zanari with fire in his eyes. The human warrior grabs his machete from his side and charges at the creature.

Zanari and Dante reach Gorvin and the human slashes at the enemy with a battle scream. The Prince gives up and lets his inner creature take over. He transformed quickly this time and strikes the creature across his face.

With a few wounds, the King became slower. Dante and Beast-Zanari push the King away as Isanto and Jorgo re-join the fight, moving away from Aries's grave.

Isanto and Zanari have killed enough creatures then they start focusing solely on the King himself.

Gorvin lifts his chest and speeds to them in a quick sprint, throwing his right arm back to slash at Isanto.

The huge wizard narrowly dodges the blow, but cannot recover fast enough to attack. Zanari lands a blow to King Gorvin's left side, punching him hard. But the punch doesn't faze his large body, and the Quinoragoras King punches the Damonarian Prince's face in a downwards motion.

Blood pours out of his nose, but Isanto grabs the King's arm before he can have another swing. The wizard enchants vines to erupt from the ground and surround the King. The vines barely hold his gigantic figure, and the warriors realize too late what the Quinoragoras King whispers on his way to the ground.

The King finished a spell from before.

Redileon, Galacieon, and Virlores burst out of the greyed out desert sands, grabbing onto Zanari, Sa'Raina, and Xanpo.

SA'RAINA. Get away from me!!!!

ZANARI. *Moving around in a panic while growling loud.* Unhand me!!

REDILEON. Heh-heh. Ya' miss me? Now you are ours to finish!!

ISANTO. *In shock.* Where could he have learned this dark sorcery?

Jorgo glances at the undead Quinoragoras Generals' in disbelief. With a loss of concentration, Isanto's vines quickly lose their hold of the King. Isanto and Jorgo, not intentional but at the same time, turn the three Generals' into stone. The stones resemble small rocky relics, easily to fit in your hand.

The three warriors, who were grabbed by the revived Generals' were free.

SA'RAINA. Thank you… *Eyes bulge out.* Look out!!!!

Isanto turns in time to see the King out of his bonds.

GORVIN. Oh… That has made me angry.

The King scratches Isanto's face, leaving a large deep scar and lots of blood came gushing out.

SA'RAINA. *Screams.* Isanto!!!!!!!!

JORGO. NOOOOOOOOOOOO!!!! *His heart immediately sank to the bottom of his soul.*

The mutilated wizard staggered back, wisps of magical energy started escaping from his body. Gorvin lightly pushed Isanto's corpse to the ground. He fell on his back.

Jorgo speeds closer to Gorvin and starts dueling the Quinoragoras King with his fists. Filled with rage, he kept on with the onslaught of furious attacks.

During the extreme and intense, violent assault he summoned enchanted vines without even saying a word. They gripped the King tight and held him as Jorgo continued pulverizing him.

Xanpo attempts to get to Jorgo's side and assist, but he's preoccupied with two other Quinoragoras. He's clawed twice, getting slashed across his chest.

Sa'Raina joins Zanari on the ground. Just then, one vine wraps around her throat by mistake and starts tightening.

Xanpo appears, not in beast form anymore. He fiercely uses his ax and slashes one of Jorgo's wild vines.

ZANARI. *On one knee, trying to control the inner beast from taking over completely.* Sa'Raina! Ahhh… Xanpo!

JORGO. *Yelling out in rage.* AHHHHH!!! **BARGO EXCAMEI!!!!!!!!** *He manages to blast the creatures away, using uncontrolled force he mistakenly obliterated a huge number of them.* No interference.

Four warriors run toward Jorgo's position, who has the King trapped in vines as he's attacking viciously. He has lost control because of Isanto's demise.

Jorgo is suddenly struck in his chest but still holds on as the King erupts in anger, angrily shouting at high decibels. The vines disintegrate and Jorgo quickly draws out a magic-based bow. He prepares to shoot Gorvin as soon as he comes out of his temper-tantrum yelling.

GORVIN. *Shouting loud.* YOU WILL NEVER WIN!!!!!!!!!!!!!!

The Damonarian Prince narrowly dodges the King's savage retaliation blows, but cannot recover or keep himself in control of his inner beast fast enough to withstand defensive attacks.

The last remaining wizard uses energy waves and manages to topple the King, making him splutter and fall.

The force of his outraged wizardry attack forces himself to the ground, partially because he's still feeling the loss for his fallen Xeiar Brother's lives. Jorgo manages to stand up and the wizard enchants vines to erupt from the ground and surround the King.

The human warriors join in and fire their blasters at the King. The vines barely hold the gigantic figure.

Sa'Raina can be heard running to the battle, shouting to her friends not to give up. She joins the battle. Their hope to take down the King by attacking from all angles increased.

XANPO. *Says in his mind.* Hopefully one of us can get through to pierce his unguarded heart.

The King suddenly smiles, making the warrior's skin crawl. He stands up from one knee thanks to the force of their attacks and whispers into his palm.

The ground under them begins to crumble. A scream was heard in the distance and the warriors all look towards the sound.

With a loss of concentration, the vines quickly lose their hold of the King.

GORVIN. *Growls and then starts chuckling.* Heh-heh.

XANPO. *Sixth sense feeling he gasps.* Watch out!!!! *He shouted to his wizard pal.*

It was too late. Jorgo had been pierced by large and sharp-pointed rocks that extended from the ground. His body lay erect but stuck on the new mountain tops.

XANPO. *He yells out.* NO!!!!!!!!!!!

SA'RAINA. Xanpo, look out!! *She rushes forward and her battle-scarred dull weapon clashes with Gorvin's claws.*

CRYST. *His neck fully healed as he's staring down at the relics that the three Quinoragoras generals were turned into. Tightening his fists.* There... You'll remain. You filthy wiz– *Hate for Jorgo was forgiven as he laid eyes on his corpse. He turns his head towards the others.*

The King has knocked Sa'Raina to the ground and is attacking Sky, Dante, and Xanpo.

GORVIN. Oh... You all... Make me... Very angry!!!! *He shouted in complete rage as he thrashed the heroes, bombarding them with fierce blows.*

The King scratches Dante's face, leaving a large scar and lots of blood. He's now lying on the ground unconscious.

SA'RAINA. *Lying on the ground, panting hard.* D – Dante!!!! *She's too weak to get up and faints.*

A piece of large flying rubble strikes Cryst in the leg. He staggers forward, eyeing the wizard's used enchanted vines and thought about a plan. He picks a few up, loosely handling them in his right hand while watching the King trying to kill more of his comrades.

Zanari is aggressively fighting the inner beast inside of him while suffering from his battle wounds.

Gorvin's claws swing twice, slashing Xanpo in the chest. Sky joins Sa'Raina on the ground, both panting pretty hard and very near death's door.

Suddenly, a faint Damonarian battle cry can be heard in the distance vastly approaching.

CRYST. *He appears behind Gorvin and jumps on his back in a rage, wrapping the vines around his neck and starts choking him. He shouts.* Zanari!!!! *Groans.* Xanpo!!!! *Struggling not to be thrown off of a rampaging monster.*

Xanpo summons enough of his remaining strength and he speed-runs towards Gorvin in a rage. He rains a series of blows on the King's right oblique. He bounces back after every fifth jab. The punches and choking only seem to be angering the King, yet Cryst is too determined and strong to let large hands swipe him off the creature's back.

Fifteen seconds pass...

The warrior, Cryst, slides down the creatures back and digs his newly extracted claws into Gorvin's rib cage. The King roared in painful agony. The massively, large King of the Quinoragoras quickly and effectively flips Cryst on his back. He brings his foot high and stomps down on the Damonarian's chest. A loud gasp was heard. Zanari, recovering from his inner beast takeover, came charging and jumped, landing on the King's back and grabbed the one vine still wrapped around the King's throat. It tightens, even more, choking him tighter. He starts turning in different darker shades of grey.

The King weighed down by Zanari's attempts to fling his body forward. Cryst, being struck and killed by the giant's large and heavy foot, brings Xanpo into a rage and he grabs Jorgo's blade off the ground. He speed-runs and slashes at his neck. Zanari was thrown before the blade made contact. He goes flying towards a large rock, and upon hearing a loud crunch as his body lands, the King chuckles as he breathed his last breath and his head fell to the ground and rolled past Cryst's corpse.

XANPO. *Turns to see where the Prince ended up.* Zanari!! *He drops Jorgo's blade and goes to the large rock.*

The Prince's body hit the ground, although he's in no condition to walk on his own.

The dead warriors lie against blood-stained rocks. Isanto and Cryst are by far the worst to view. Xanpo drops his stare, looking at Gorvin's head at the river's edge and then he looks over at the three generals' relics. He starts walking to them.

XANPO. *Raises his head toward the river and notices wizardry, sparkly lights emanating from Gorvin's now floating head.* What in the – *His right hand resting on the three relics, but paying attention to Gorvin's head.*

He's sure to be dead, but it starts speaking in a daunting tone of voice.

GORVIN. *Blood spurts out of his mouth and he whispers in a dry and raspy voice.* Finally… defeated. But you have not won… *His blackened eyes roll to the back of his head and his entire head starts shrinking and turns to dust.*

Ten minutes later....

Xanpo and the remaining warriors, majority human, are still at the battleground where they are mourning their friends. Itisa contacted the group, appearing by a visual television cloud, and told them how they have just ended the war. But there's no time to celebrate.

There's four relics left behind. Two humans are unconscious, one suffers from a bruised rib cage, and two Damonarians are somewhat conscious but awake.

XANPO. *Breathing hard.* I – I won't leave these here.

ZANARI. *Coughs harsh.* Take 'em… *Coughs twice and spits a small pool of blood on the dirt.* –to Xeiar.

XANPO. I d – don't think that will fly by the Great Xeiars. *Pauses for a few seconds to see straight.* They moved their planet just before the war started.

ZANARI. *Lying face to the dirt, clutching his chest.* Possibly there's another place. *Coughs harsh and rolls on his back.*

XANPO. *Struggles to get off the dirt and approach the relics.* Nah. We find a way to destroy those right here, right now!! There's definite dark magic that was done beforehand.

CRYSTALIA. *Appearing in a ball of purple smoke out of the blue.* Then we try again!

Zanari groans while losing his balance and collapses on the dirt.

ITISA. *Emerges out of the ball of smoke.* They will be taken back to their respective homes. Young Liesean here will handle that task.

CRYSTALIA. Yes, Itisa.

ITISA. Earth… it should be. For a short time. *Coughs.* There was a temporary non-government experimental laboratory near Niechest Town. Xanpo. You take it there and we'll discover how to destroy those relics for good before those four creatures manage to revive themselves. I've checked it out. I have borrowed sacred spells to create powerful shields that'll keep the relics from being discovered. Neirolo Cavern will have some of the best enchanted, impenetrable defenses.

XANPO. *Eyeing Jorgo's blade near his right foot and looks at his mentor.* Can Xeiarian steel penetrate it?

ITISA. I believe that's not possible.

XANPO. *Shaking his head.* Well without a Transporter Roon or a Transporter Relic we're stuck here. *Sighs and looks to the darkened, foreign sky. He murmurs.* I was told to look out for two youngsters.

ITISA. *Hearing but not showing she knows who Xanpo is talking about.* I'm sure you'll make it back in time. *Facing the dark waters, she sighs and turns, facing Xanpo.* There's another thing I'll need you to do after we take the relics to Earth.

XANPO. I'm listening. What do you need?

ITISA. After the task is done, I'll let you know. *Turns and nods to Crystalia.* Let us go to Earth.

CRYSTALIA. *Preparing to do the trans-dimensional spell. Turns to look at the warrior.* Although I believe Jorgo's blade suits you, why are you still holding onto his weapon?

XANPO. *Not showing any emotion.* Why bury a perfectly useful weapon? *Smiles.*

SCENE SHIFTS TO PLANET EARTH
IN THE ISOLATED DIMENSION

Xanpo walked the relics deep inside Neirolo Cavern. Itisa and Crystalia waited for him. The moment Xanpo stepped outside, the sorceress and witch placed many incantations on the cavern. They departed to their respective homes soon after.

This next part of the series shifts forward in time to current battles with the revived Quinoragoras Generals. Niara, Akiru, and Christen were joined by Zanari and Sky.

Elsewhere, a mile away from Neirolo Cavern, DaGoru has found Xanpo lurking around the area. Xanpo is searching all around Neichest for any possible indications to how the Generals' escaped. He's remembering the incantations Itisa had done on the cavern years ago, noticing they're no longer in place.

XANPO. That's – Not possible. *Sighs.* Those teenagers possibly triggered something in Itisa's spell to counteract its effectiveness. Either that... Or? *An idea pops into his head.* Viera. Heh. She's free. *Shakes his head twice.* Now we'll ha – *Using quick reflexes jumps up and away from the spot where he was standing and lands a few paces back.* That was close. *Stares in the direction where the blast came from.* You again. *He raises his voice.* Your wizard master order you to finish the job?

DAGORU. *Walking at a normal pace, sword over his head toward the Damonarian warrior.* I have no master.

Xanpo stood alert, his attention fixed on the creature that stood before him, puffing and fuming as if, somehow, he had already made up a grudge.

He studied the creature; a man fused with one of those creatures from planet Xeiar. He had always seen and battled within the recent past, training with Itisa. Some locals, Xeiarians, say that this breed of creature is fierce. Xanpo had heard the rumors about all the supernatural beasts in Namorant. Word had it – It was possible to beat them if one was lucky enough to discover their weak points. Now Xanpo tried his best to find this vulnerability in this fused creature grunting before him, but nothing in it resembled a weakness.

Its muscles looked huge and thick like they were made of metal fibers. The hair behind his back was alert just as his eyes were. DaGoru looked like a tough fighter, and judging from the way he maintained a relaxed pose, Xanpo knew that he must also be an experienced fighter. The human warrior was still trying to find a weak point in DaGoru's body that in overall looked like armor by itself.

DaGoru seemed tired of waiting for his opponent to make the first attack. He looked impatient. Raising his arms and letting out a loud growl, the warrior banged on his chest several times before charging at Xanpo at lightning speed, his fists raised to flaunt impressive claws sprouting from his fingernails. Xanpo stood steadily in his warrior's outfit. He had been expecting him to make the first move, so that did not take him by surprise at all.

He swayed a little to the right, missing DaGoru's fist by a few inches. He felt the air rush against his cheeks as DaGoru followed the direction of his blow. Xanpo turned to face his opponent, his tail now standing alert and his right arm on his blade (once belonged to the deceased warrior Jorgo). He was ready.

DaGoru was quick to notice Xanpo's grip on his weapon. He didn't wait for him to strike. He knew that if he waited for the warrior to draw his blade, the battle was as good as over. Sprinting again towards Xanpo, DaGoru slid towards him, aiming for his legs. Xanpo had drawn his blade halfway out of its sheath when DaGoru slid into his feet, upsetting him and sending him spluttering to the ground, losing the grip on his weapon which went flying meters away.

DaGoru was up in seconds, grinning at his accomplishment in disarming him.

Xanpo struggled to his feet slowly. He had to come up with an alternative plan of beating his rival now. He just needed time to figure it out. He was barely on his feet when DaGoru's fist came flying. This strike caught Xanpo off-guard just like the previous one, landing squarely on his left jaw and sending him to his knees. He spat blood from his mouth. He realized now that the fighter he was facing was on another level. His speed and strength were something to be worried about especially now that he didn't have his blade. Apart from this, however, something else was bothering him; something about this fighter seemed familiar, almost too familiar as if they had fought before. Xanpo put the thought aside though; after all, he had fought thousands of fighters in his life. Who cared if some of them fought the same way, right?

Slowly, he got to his feet, wiped the dust off his outfit, stretched his neck and clenched his fists. It was time for DaGoru to have a taste of the famous Xanpo. DaGoru was circling him now, making sudden movements toward him, looking for a chance to attack. Xanpo stayed calm, following DaGoru's movements with his eyes, observing every step he took, trying to detect a pattern. When he did, DaGoru wasn't waiting for what came next. Sprinting towards him, Xanpo let DaGoru sway dangerously to avoid being hit. Little did he know that this was just a set up for the real attack. No sooner had the fused creature lost his balance in his effort to dodge than Xanpo applied the real attack, bringing his right foot down hard against DaGoru's forehead, forcing him to land on the ground with a thud. Seizing this opportunity, Xanpo went down on the fallen creature, raining heavy blows to his head and ducking the claws that came aiming for his eyes. When he was sure that he had had enough, Xanpo stood up. He was sure now that DaGoru had gotten the message; this wasn't going to end up so nicely for him.

DaGoru stood up, staggered for a while as he struggled to regain his balance. His head was ringing now and he was partially blinded by blood that was oozing from his forehead. Xanpo observed him staying composed and waiting for him to recover. DaGoru was outrageous now. Little did he know that all this was part of Xanpo's plan. He knew that fighting furiously meant fighting carelessly, and that's what he planned to use against this beast. He had already found its weak spot – the head – now all he needed was a chance to get to it.

DaGoru's first furious attack came sooner than Xanpo had anticipated, but he was ready for it altogether. It was a right punch, targeting Xanpo's chest. Xanpo easily blocked it. Taking hold of DaGoru's index finger and carefully avoiding the sharp claws, Xanpo bent it backwards, taking the entire wrist with it. The creature screamed in pain and he went down on one knee.

XANPO. Heh. Perfect! *He smiled.*

The right side of his head now remained unprotected, and his left arm was already too busy trying to free its trapped partner. Lifting his fists high, Xanpo sent a powerful jab directly to DaGoru's face, his biceps vibrating at the impact as his fist crashed into DaGoru's jaw. He felt the jawbone crack. Two more punches and Xanpo felt DaGoru's body become limp. He raised his fist again ready for the final blow but stopped midair, his entire arm shaking as he repressed the urge to finish off his opponent. He let go of him and DaGoru slumped to the ground.

Xanpo looked at the injured creature indifferently then walked slowly to where his blade was. He picked it up, gave DaGoru a last glance before sliding it back to its sheath and walking off.

The half-Damonarian warrior had only walked off for a few meters when a blinding flash of light seemingly out of thin air appeared before him. He stopped suddenly and went for his blade. This time, he didn't have to guess who his opponent.

The Xeiar wizards were a well-known breed of fighters who used magic and martial arts to fight. They were fierce, and to defeat them would be a far-fetched expectation.

He could still feel the pain in his chest and jaws from his previous fight just a few moments ago, yet this was not the kind of battle he was willing to simply flee from.

Xanpo watched as the light dimmed down, gradually settling into a human image. When it disappeared Maleena was visible, hovering in the sky, her head bowed down and her right hand resting at her side. She was exposing her wizardly wand from where the light was coming from.

Xanpo knew that the stance meant war and unlike other opponents he faced, he couldn't let this one make the first move. He knew his warrior side would not be as strong against the wizard as his human side. He had to find a way to fight her magic even if it meant death.

Quickly, he performed a swift trick, hurling his blade into the air in a bid to distract the wizard's attention, before transforming to his beastly form and charging forward full speed. He was just about to land a devastating hit on his target when out of nowhere, the light emerged again, this time with a physical force that pushed him so hard that he went flying back like he weighed less than a pound. The blade came catapulting towards him, the pointy end first. He was lucky to notice it as it landed just a few inches from his chest.

The male warrior stood up, furious. Ignoring his weapon, he now sprinted towards the wizard, who was now on the ground in her kneeling position, obviously unbothered by the warrior's fury. Seconds later, Xanpo was back on the ground, only this time he found himself a bit further, and with a serious injury on his left shoulder after landing badly on a tree stump. He tried to pick himself up but he couldn't. Maleena had stood up now, and Xanpo knew that he was trapped.

She raised her right arm, the light from the glowing wand becoming brighter. Xanpo closed his eyes, expecting the worst. From a distance, he heard the loud bang as the wizard released her pink emblazoned attack like a blow. Almost at the same time, Xanpo felt his body being lifted and tossed away by an unknown force. He opened his eyes just in time to see the pink residue from the attack land on the place he had been lying just a second ago, reducing everything from the trees to the stumps into dust and ashes.

He looked up to see the detective, Nolan, looking down at him, shouting some inaudible words. Next to him was Officer Sa'Raina and the young Agent Eron dodging several spell blasts. Xanpo had fought with these three before.

NOLAN. You're okay. *He said without turning to look.*

He afforded a nod as he tried to rise. Sa'Raina helped him to his feet and they stood in position, facing the female wizard after she shot a spell at the young agent, sending him crashing into a nearby tree stump. She gazed at the three, standing on her feet, fireballs burning from both her hands. Eron was barely capable of walking to the others. In a split of a second, the group of four was charging, screaming at the top of their voices.

Maleena gave them time to get near her then letting out a huge shriek too, she released the pair of fireballs from her special wand, both missing the group just by a whisker, but their impact too strong that it threw them high into the air like feathers in a hurricane before landing hard on a huge tree trunk and falling on top of each other like bags in a store. She raised her hands ready to strike again but none of the four bodies moved. She stared at them for a moment then as if she had done nothing, her body lit up in a pink flash of light.

It happened incredibly fast!

The place became quiet, a type of calmness that only comes after a huge bang; the kind that left a tense atmosphere, as if another noise would erupt from the thin air and disrupt the fragile peace.

It was in this quietness that Maleena lay sprawled out on the hard, dirty ground, motionless and lifeless. A huge gaping hole in the middle of her back. Her left arm was still slightly raised as if she was still trying to shield her body from the fatal blow that had cost her life to be surprisingly taken. Her face was covered in blood and half-buried in the dirt. Her weapon lay next to her, handle drenched in the blood such that the only part visible was the very bottom of the hilt.

The silence of the environment around her and the stillness of her body brought an eerie feeling.

Not everything was so silent though.

Standing triumphantly above Maleena, high in the sky above, breathing slowly in gasps, Red-Eye gazed down at what could have been a fierce rival just a few moments ago.

Red-Eye grunted as he watched blood oozing from the dead woman's neck and the upper section of her back. His huge nostrils twitched as he took in heavy tufts of air.

He raised his hands for a moment to touch his horns; bloodying them slightly, only the bloodstains weren't noticeable due to the red color of the horns.

Red-Eye looked down at his huge chest, heaving up and down beneath the red armor he had as thick layers of skin. His long muscular arms moved in rhythm with the rest of his body, his fingers were spread wide, displaying the fierce sharp claws growing from their tips. He closed his eyes as if to enjoy the sudden silence. His moment of triumph was short-lived; however, for out of the horizon, footsteps were approaching; quick, powerful footsteps. Red-Eye knew better than to continue enjoying his comfort zone. He realized now he had won a battle, but the war was far from over.

Red-Eye stood upright and turned to face his new threat. His long tail swayed with his body, then stood upright in anticipation. He could feel the adrenaline spread through his blood veins again, like a wildfire burning into his body. He knew that this challenger was more than the one he had put down, yet he was not scared; he was excited. He had lived his entire life fighting before being trapped in a relic for what felt like centuries. He was itching for a good fight. This was what he enjoyed doing.

He looked at the figure approaching him at a threatening speed and he smiled a cruel, menacing smile.

Asarios was a young man, possibly in his twenties, with a lean body and equally slim features. His dark hair was slightly messy and it blew up in the wind as he walked. He wore a slim pair of pants and a blue shirt that looked a little too tight for him, working perfectly to expose his well-built body. Carefully perched on his back was a sword that hangs on a sheath, swinging dangerously from side-to-side as he sped off towards the creature standing a few paces in front of him.

ASARIOS. *Noticing the body on the ground, he increased his pace.* NO!! N – This isn't happening. *He whispered to himself between clenched teeth.*

Maleena's body was now in full sight. Asarios knew from the sight that she was dead. Red-Eye saw the devastated look on the wizard's face and grinned. He knew that beating an angry opponent would be exhilarating fun.

He now stood ready to attack as Asarios closed in on him. Red-Eye raised his right arm, his claws ready to catch anything that missed the rest of the arm.

Asarios was now mad with fury. His eyes were partially blinded. All he saw was the body on the ground. If only he had arrived a few minutes earlier... Red-Eye was now a few paces ahead. He looked ready to pounce. Asarios cleared his mind and in a split of a moment, he let his body dive headfirst into the ground, sliding in between Red-Eye's feet and evading the deadly blow that the beast had aimed at his chest. At the same time, the wizard took his sword and managed to bruise Red-Eye's tail.

The creature was pushed by the eight of his blows. He staggered off a few meters away and stopped. Asarios was leaning beside the female wizard's body. Red-Eye noticed his vulnerable position and began approaching him, getting ready for the second strike. He moved on towards his target steadily, only to be stopped by a sudden light that came from Maleena's body.

He had not seen this kind of scenario before. The light was impeccably blinding that he had to shield his eyes from it. It seemed to have completely covered Asarios, who trotted away from the body, taken aback too by this sudden change. Red-Eye thought he saw Asarios's form change multiple times, but from where he stood, it only looked like a silhouette figure probably playing games with his vision.

His dead friend's body's fatal wound, there was a hole in her back. Magical pink light came gushing... taking him by surprise. Before he could even comprehend what was happening, a sharp pain ran through his head. Like a thousand needles were trapped in his blood. His eyes were blinded instantly and his entire body was submerged in this light that felt like a pot of boiling acid. He opened his mouth and a loud shriek came out, upsetting the silence that had begun to form once more. He knew what such pain meant, and it was clear now that he had to fight whatever was happening to him before he could face the monster he so much wanted to kill. He felt the beast in him arise, like a demon that had been cast away for years, finally resurrecting and rising with the fire.

Asarios's hair was already beginning to transform. His wavy, light hair beginning to shrink and harden like fur. He could feel the skin around his head and face starting to enlarge too, like someone was passing hot metal on it, ironing it out and forcing it to take another form. His bones followed suit, breaking and rejoining, stretching and dwindling at the same time. His facial features changed. His arms were now starting to change, nails stretching out into large sharp claws. His feet were already covered in slime.

He didn't think Maleena's powers were meant to strengthen him, but if he allowed this beast to get out there... it would be no controlling it. He knew that he now had to harness Maleena's face and at the same time fight to maintain his human form.

Slowly, he let out one last scream and bit his lower lip. He had to win this. He closed his eyes in agony as the fire continued burning through his veins into the muscles. He tried to keep his mind calm, ignoring all the pain and trying to focus on losing control of his physical form. He felt the bones revert to their original form, experiencing the same pain in reverse. Finally, he gasped in relief as the fire burned out gradually. He opened his eyes slowly. His body was normal. Only super psyched. He felt like he had the energy of a thousand men in him. The creature standing before him now seemed less scary. He couldn't wait to avenge his friend.

Red-Eye observed his opponent, trying hard not to show his astonishment. Honestly, the incident had taken him back and even though he didn't show it, he was a little bit shaken.

RED-EYE. *Thinking hard and out loud.* He must've gotten into Valdesmon somehow. The amount of dark, evil souls in the place would be enou– *Gasps.* No. Could he have absorbed those lost powers making it his own? *Eyes bulging out of his sockets, completely worried and shocked.* Could he? *He's pondering.*

He clenched his fists and starts approaching Asarios, who's waiting, sword in his right hand.

ASARIOS. *Speaking out loud to himself.* Not today. Her powers must be helping that power to not consume my soul.

Shaking away his thoughts and reacts. He was the first one to strike, swinging his sword fiercely, aiming for Red-Eye's right fist. The creature managed to dodge this strike by hitting the sword by its side and managing to steer it from its target. The strike left a bruise on his fist. He stopped to examine his injury. Asarios was motivated now. He raised his sword and prepared his next move, eyeing the enemy from the corners of his eyes. Red-Eye's excited. He has a worthy rival.

He moves slowly towards him, showing no sign of the attack he was planning on next. A few inches from Asarios, he jumped, aiming a flying kick that caught him straight to the jaw, sending him flying off and landing on the ground sputtering blood from his mouth. He hadn't seen that coming. Now as he got up, he knew that this would be a hard battle. He hardened the grip on his sword and approached Red-Eye, who was waiting, expressionless, doing all he could not to betray his next move.

Asarios tried to figure out Red-Eye's game, swinging his sword in several stunts and throwing a few serious to confuse the big guy but nothing worked. He found himself down each time. Red-Eye seemed to have a thousand surprise attacks planned out.

The lone wizard was beginning to get desperate now and he felt fury come over him. This beast had killed his only companion and it now threatened to finish him off. Angrily he got up from his beaten position and started somersaulting above Red-Eye; he attempted to strike from above him.

The sword reached its target this time, but it did nothing to hurt him, who stretched his long arms, catching Asarios in the air and brought him down to the ground at lightning speed. The wizard's world went black for a moment. The fury was unbearable now. He felt Maleena's fire starting to burn inside him again. His bones were beginning to transform, only this time he wasn't sure he could control it. He tried to get up, but his hands were in the middle of a transformation and they couldn't support him. He looked at Red-Eye. He was standing a few meters away, observing the happenings in awe. Suddenly, Asarios had an idea. He realized he had an advantage of Maleena's power being cooped up inside him. He could use this to beat Red-Eye. Slowly, he closed his eyes and stood up, allowing the transformation to take control for the moment. Red-Eye was startled and he took a few steps behind, not sure about what to do. Asarios staggered towards him, shrieking in pain while timing his attack. Red-Eye noticed that his rival was in a helpless state and stopped.

This was the moment Asarios had been waiting for. Red-Eye had let down his guard. Swiftly, Asarios reached for his sword, and at the same time repressing the transformation. This time, he swung his sword with the agility of a thousand soldiers, aiming it at the beast's neck.

In a blink of an eye, Red-Eye's head had dropped to the ground, as a human teenager's body spiritually pulled out of the creature. The creature's head was rolling a few times before coming to a stop a few inches away from Maleena's body. Almost as if the two species were of complete opposites of each other. The rest of the body followed, kneeling at first before losing balance and falling like an empty sack.

The wizard laid eyes at the human being who was now lying on the ground next to the creature's body minus the decapitated head. Luckily whatever caused them to become one, wore off before the human was decapitated as well.

ASARIOS. Didn't know I'd knew how hard the Quinoragoras's skin to be. *Spits blood on the ground.* There was no need for using spells on you.

Crebeon and Pichuel successfully transported the rest of the heroes to Asarios's current location. Donny, Sally, Namina, Saber, NiKoLee, and a Super-Charged Max Telguaso are ready to take on the wizard. Saber has new armor on, utilizing one of SAB AI's modes; the Defense Maneuver 00 Fusion. Using this mode, she also has access to maneuvers 09, 10, 11, and 12.

Beast-Zanari is heard coming into view racing to the place carrying Niara on his back, with two Super-Charged cross-humans: Beast-Christen and Beast-Akiru running alongside him. Each cross-human having Vexion creatures maximizing their full potential.

SABER. *Right fist tightening around her staff and she scans the battlefield.* Oh no. Mom!!!! *She runs over to her mother's body and drops to her knees.* Mama! Wake up, please!!!!

ASARIOS. *Eyes look to the human girl.* Now you see why I had to exterminate that filthy species. *Eyes move to Maleena's body.* Your emotions are quite similar.

SABER. *Voice loud and strong.* WHAT DID YOU SAY?!! *Wipes her eyes clean and stands up, gripping her weapon tight and staring daggers at the wizard.* Did you do this?!!

XANPO. *Shouts across the field.* Saber!! That wasn't him. Calm yourself right now.

Akiru and Max, on all fours, run to and gets in front of her.

DONNY and SALLY. *In a whisper.* Our attacks won't work
on him.

SALLY. His aura is totally off compared to other Xeiarians.

DONNY. Even our spells weren't powerful enough to stop
those creatures. Xanpo's will to fight is like one in a
few that might be able to hurt him.

SALLY. Maybe we should give our abilities to him.

XANPO. *Caught the whisper. He turns his head slightly to the left
and whispers back.* I would gladly accept them, but it
doesn't work that way. *He smiles and looks out in front of
him.* I've trained you both! Yourself Donny has been
trained a year longer than Sally. You, Sally, have
been to another world and came back even stronger.
Soft chuckle. I know you two can do this!

The two young wizards look at the intimidating wizard
then notice the two beast cross-human boys biting Saber's
clothing to stop her from advancing on to fight Asarios
alone. Xanpo quick-steps in front of a stubborn nature Saber
and the two boys stop biting her clothing.

XANPO. We'll do this together, right?

SABER. *Rolls her eyes.* All right, whatever. But I get the
finishing blow!!

ASARIOS. *Dull and annoyed tone.* Pretty sure that pleasure will be inconclusive. *Arms out to the side.* Stop talking and stop me. *Drops his arms to his sides.* I'll get my revenge no matter who shows up.

XANPO. You've killed Redileon! I don't get it!! What revenge do you speak?!

ASARIOS. *Squints his eyes and looking distasteful at the warrior Xanpo.* You're starting to irk me. *Sighs.* But I did feel him here – on this world a while ago. He was here!

ZANARI. *Growling.* The Great. He's talking about one of the Greats.

XANPO. *Turns and stares, for only seconds, at the controlled beast form of Zanari.* This is about Xeiar? Why is he here on Earth then?

ASARIOS. Those legendary wizards over there. Myself and– *Shakes away the thoughts of his fallen friend and grows silent.* Enough. *Shakes his head.* I'm done explaining – Hoping – Wishing!! *Shouts.* Are YOU READY?!!! *He powers up. The feel of dreadful power causes his opponents to take a step back and the children to flinch. He clenches both fists.*

Approximately thirty paces away from the battle, Dante (as DaGoru) leans over and watches the fiery teen boy. He feels in his heart that that's Akiru, his nephew. He's trying to gather strength to save his brother's boy and the boy's friends, but the strain on this body isn't allowing him to stand.

With blinding speed, Xanpo Quick-Steps to Asarios only to be forced to the ground by a seemingly light brush off.

Asarios is standing over Xanpo who has fallen on his knees. He looks down at him and lifts his hand. Xanpo begins to choke and struggles to breathe. He couldn't believe it! Wow! What an attack.

A sixth sense. The wizard uses his peripheral vision, eyes moving to the left. A blazing stream of fire is headed in his direction.

ASARIOS. *Quick response.* **DEPARO RITAMEH!!**

The fused beast, DaGoru, starts writhing in pain and drops to his knees. The attack was reversed and struck the user directly in his chest.

Seconds pass and fire lift off the fused being, revealing Dante Skalizer's human self. He has stopped yelling at this time. Akiru's eyes widened. He became shocked to see his uncle.

BEAST-AKIRU. *Light whispers.* Dante–

XANPO. *Slowly, but cautiously getting to his feet.* No. How didn't I realize it was you this entire time? *At a loss for words.*

ASARIOS. *He lowers his arms, staring at the dying man.* You – I made you stronger. The beast I created in that dimension. Came here. You stopped it and fused with it. Now – You try and hurt me? *He raises his right arm and snaps two fingers.* **Ritmir.**

Dante has become dead silent. He's staring up and seconds later falls without making any sound. The nephew doesn't know what to do. His mind has become blank as he's staring at his fallen relative.

Asari's innocence is pulled back to reality, brought back for a tiny bit. His body is facing the fallen human, but in his mind, he's elsewhere.

The wizard is a boy again, Asari. He's standing on a cliff, looking out at magical creatures flying around. He's smiling. He turns and sees the Quinoragoras child Kweezan to his left and turns to his right and sees Malee smiling back at him with her eyes closed. He's happy.

ASARIOS. *In thought.* What is this? *Confused.*

Suddenly, Asarios is pulled back to reality and is lifted ten feet in the air by a giant wolf-like beast. The beast is a Damonarian, i.e. Zanari.

A rageful smoke erupts from Beast-Zanari's nose as he glares at the wizard who saved himself using tree vines.

ASARIOS. Is that all you got? *Mockingly to Zanari then shoots ice spikes at him.*

The Prince can dodge it all the while charging at the evil wizard. A few of the materialized ice spikes cut and brush past him though.

Meanwhile, hiding in a tree incognito….

ZOEY. Are we waiting for a few more minutes? I don't think they'll last any longer.

KASE. *On edge, staring down at the heroes fighting that strange man as fear coursing through her. She gulps and catches what her friend whispered.* I'm – Ahem. A few more minutes, Zoey.

Asarios is taken aback when Beast-Zanari lets out a howl and whacks him with his large head. The wizard loses his balance and slides back. He bangs his head on the dense tree trunk, but just when he was about to blast a fireball to burn Beast-Zanari to ashes, the young wizard Donny freezes the fireball attack and Niara obliterates it with her mind.

ASARIOS. *Turns his attention to the two youngsters.* You filthy creatures will never defeat me! *He gets up and snaps his fingers.*

At once, the sky rumbles and roars. Bolts of energy blast directly at Donny and Namina, throwing them away from the evil wizard. The two struggle to stand, having trouble with their breathing and stamina.

Xanpo gets up and turns into his gigantic Damonarian beast form, with fangs like a Hyenas.

BEAST-ZANARI. Xanpo!! *Shouts across the open area.* Will you be okay? *Asked worriedly.*

BEAST-XANPO. *Eyes glued on the evil wizard.* Don't worry about me. *He breathed.* Let's keep our minds focused on defeating this foe.

Beast-Zanari nods and the two readied themselves to charge at him.

Sally, who was hiding in the shadow along with Namina, comes out and paralyzes Asarios in surprise. Sally has a created magical barrier for Saber, Donny, and Niara who are lying insensible.

Asarios struggles to use his limbs. He tries to use his fingers to create a spell, but Pichuel flies towards him and throws a ball made of electricity at him. The wizard grits his teeth in pain, but he quickly withstands the attack and repels the remaining energy right at helpless Namina.

Crebeon appears, protecting the girl, and shoots an energy blast turning the energy into sparkles. Namina is saved.

BEAST-XANPO. This won't do! *Speaking in frustration.* We must round him up!

Max, who shifts into his fused beast form, has no problems, hovers down at Asarios and uses his panther-like claws to strike. Asarios lets out a yelp and materializes his magic sword that emits shades of blue and silver and black. He jabs it above him as Beast-Max passes, stabbing him in his oblique muscle. He shoots like an electric rocket, plummeting to the dirt ground.

Sally is standing a few paces away, manipulating the Earth around. Giant soil pillars emerge from underneath and surround Asarios.

Zanari rubs his hoofs on the soil and charges at Asarios. Xanpo follows, but the two of them are stopped as the ground liquidates.

BEAST-ZANARI. *Oblivious to what Sally is doing.* What the hell…? *He mumbles.*

Beast-Xanpo and Beast-Zanari gradually sink.

BEAST-CHRISTEN. *Shouts and orders.* Everyone, cover your ears!! *Lets out a shriek that rang Asarios' eardrum and should've cracked his sword but didn't.*

Beast-Akiru, full of rage and a look of revenge, galloped toward Asarios, who was unable to think properly because of Niara's psychic ability to hallucinate him and started circling the pillars and trapping him in a blazing fiery ring.

Asarios drops his sword on the ground, readying himself for a surprise attack from Sally.

NAMINA. *Screams out.* NiKoLee!!!! Don't go!! *Tone of voice lowers.* Come back!

NIARA. Destr – *Sees NiKoLee running away from her twin and toward the wizard.* No!!

She yelled and immediately NiKoLee halts, looked at Niara and ran back to the bushes to protect Namina.

Asarios screamed and pushed Beast-Christen away. He was infuriated and slightly hurt. Just then, Beast-Xanpo and

Beast-Zanari are brought out from the quicksand with the help of Donny.

Eventually, he had come back to his senses but was still a little weak.

BEAST-ZANARI. Asarios, stop fighting at once! *Commanding tone.*

ASARIOS. *Chuckles.* Heh-heh. No way. I'll never give up so easily. You all haven't felt pain yet! *He said and dashed at them.*

They dashed at him too and the Earth trembled violently beneath them. The massive power everyone's giving off is off the charts. Asarios created a spiky ball and chain and swung it at Beast-Xanpo and Beast-Zanari. The two were severely injured and shifted out of the beast forms.

Beast-Max and Beast-Akiru quickly speed in and punches Asarios on his right cheek. Asarios caught off guard for the split second, is taken aback. He didn't expect that move.

Max and Akiru have shifted back to their regular cross-human forms, breathing heavily, but it was no time to stop now.

Beast-Christen speeds to the wizard, hands into claws, and attacked Asarios head-on. Asarios was able to block his face from getting damaged but not his arms.

Pichuel and Crebeon shoot energy and electric blasts at Asarios from behind. Niara teleports herself right behind

Asarios and throws punches at his ribs. The wizard turns to catch her, but Niara snaps her fingers again and appears much closer, punching his nose. She snaps again and this time, she brings Sally and Donny with her.

Asarios tries to fight back with his bare hands, but Zanari blocks him and punches his left cheek. Xanpo comes back, taking the lead and pulls a quick uppercut and kick at his abdomen. Asarios falls back but doesn't give up so easily. He maneuvers the rocks to become his army but his dreams shatter when Donny along with Sally who happened to wake up, crumble his army.

ASARIOS. You two… Are like myself and Maleena. *He whispered.* Ahhh!!! *He screamed in frustration and uses both his hands to bind the little group of insects who caused him so much anguish.*

The wizard closed his fingers and they began to choke yet again. He was strangling all of them, even Niara and Sally who were trying to break Asarios suffocation curse.

BEAST-CHRISTEN. You all had fun, now it's my turn!

In time, the boy comes running like a cheetah. He had enough energy to summon his fighter cat-lings to assist. They quickly attack Asarios one by one, slapping at him almost like baby kittens playing with yarn. The scene is quite bizarre.

With the distraction, the little group is saved and they can breathe again.

Asarios tries to move away, but Beast-Christen swiftly calls the fighter cats back into his body and attacks Asarios' head-on.

BEAST-CHRISTEN. *Voice loud, strong, and confident.* This is for controlling my mind!!

ASARIOS. *Not fazed by the attacks.* You lot still think you can win…? *He smirks and tightens his grip on him.*

Zanari fears what he might do to the human. He quickly stands and launches forward only to fall on his face. He's exhausted. The rest of the team surround Asarios in a circle and wait for his next move.

ASARIOS. Enough!!!! *He choked, releasing Christen and allowing him to move away from him.* I'm going to end you all! Right here… Right now. *He closes his eyes and mumbles a spell.*

Two pre-teen girls fling themselves out of a tree and they're en route to land attacks. Donny and Saber notice the two girls.

SABER. *Voice loud.* NOT YOU TWO!!!!

DONNY. *Quick thinking.* **RESMEND QUIPISTORAH!**

No one else noticed Kase and Zoey. Donny immediately froze their pending attacks on Asarios and transported them to safety on the ground nearby.

XANPO. *His eyes grow wide and he turns to everyone.* RUNNNNNNNNNN!!!!! *He yelled out.*

But before they had the chance to react, Asarios had created a magical spear of energy from within himself and just when he opened his eyes and screamed using strong lung power, everything from the forest to the cosmos, went blindingly bright.

****

A short time after, right outside of the southern gate of Melovaton City, a school mate of Orion's has kicked his soccer ball into Melova Desert. Two other boys turn to look at each other, expressionless.

ORION COLLINS. It's okay, guys. I got it. *He starts running to the exit of the desert.*

A few minutes in, Orion notices his ball is resting near slabs of oddly shaped pieces of concrete. Weird because there were no buildings anywhere in sight.

He reaches for his ball and sees something glisten to his left, ten feet away. He picks his ball up, without taking his eyes off the object buried in sand, and walks over to it.

Orion kicks sand off the half-buried object and notices the hilt of a strange weapon. He places his ball on the ground and starts digging.

ORION COLLINS. Wow! *His eyes open wide.* How'd this get here?

Little Orion is staring at the sword in hand, eyeing the silvery weapon which has a blue hilt. It appears that it just got here somehow but from where?

The teen boy grips the weapon properly, right-hand firm on the handle. He grabs his soccer ball and starts running to the city's south gate.

****

Ruins of Pompeii. A Roman town which was destroyed by a volcanic eruption in 79AD. The preserved ancient Roman city in Campania, Italy, 14 miles (23 km) southeast of Naples, at the southeastern base of Mount Vesuvius.

This place was built, by ancient people, with help from prehistoric lava flow to the north of the mouth of the Sarnus River.

There's an Italian girl, dressed rather peculiar. She appears to be looking for someone.

An hour and some minutes earlier, she was at the nearest populated town when she saw a flash of light coming from the Ruins of Pompeii. She decided to go investigate.

A yellow feline humanoid springs out of the river and into the air. The girl takes a firm stance, preparing herself.

The yellow cat screeches and tries to claw her. She quickly maneuvers her body, taking the hand of the creature to push him to the ground. She doesn't wait for him to get up. The girl materializes an object and throws it.

This strange spiral device clings onto the feline and he goes night-night, while his form changes to a teen boy possibly around the age of fourteen years.

****

A month past. Traveling to Israel. Officer Dunan has taken a leave of absence from his Officer duties in HighTech City.

He locates his younger brother, who's patrolling a perimeter at an undisclosed location in a foreign country somewhere from the nearest water reserve.

OGDO. Heh. Well if it isn't my Big Bro! *Smiles.* Thought yo' ass was a mirage for a minute. Psst. Lucky I didn't blast your butt. What's up? HighTech running you into the ground? Heh-heh. You looking stressed as hell.

DUNAN. It's good to see you too, little brother. *Serious tone.*

OGDO. *Lifts his chin, noticing the seriousness in his brother's voice.* You good?

DUNAN. *Exhales and eyes the surroundings before meeting eyes with his brother again.* I'm going to need your assistance.

OGDO. Do you notice I'm working right now?

DUNAN. This ISCA organization. They're formidable opponents, but not a primary concern.

OGDO. Heh. Yeah. *Worried expression.* You should leave before my superiors think I'm slacking.

DUNAN. I've had a word with your chain-of-command. You are officially on leave, starting at this hour.

OGDO. Heh. Knowing you, you didn't and I'll be AWOL. *Smirks with excitement and looks very intrigued.* But you've piqued my interest. *Placing 9mm in his leg holster.* Speak to me. *Nods at his brother.* What ya' got?

DUNAN. These special-enhanced humans need certain attention.

OGDO. *Confused.* Uhhh. I take it I should know what you're talking about. Specially enhanced humans? *Looks away while joking around.* Oh man. Mama should NOT have been on the pipe when she had you in the oven. *Laughs a few seconds and stops.*

Dunan's eyes dart away and glance at the sky above. A few seconds of staring at the clouds he lowers his eyes back on his little brother and half-smiles.

OGDO. Had me there for a moment. *Shrugs.* But I'm in! You seem serious enough. What do you need from me exactly?

DUNAN. Your skills. There's no one I find as qualified to get this job done efficiently than family. *His mouth twitched unintentionally.* Due consider that these special humans are extremely dangerous.

OGDO. Hm. *Smiles.* So – Am – I. *Chuckles with right hand on his rifle. He starts taping it with his pointer-finger.*

APPENDIX 1

LOCATIONS, CITIES, TOWNS, AND STATES

Hidendale Springs, Illinois *Thirty minutes north of Dowers City, IL.*

- Hidendale Observatory *Home of an all new exhibit with twenty planets on display.*
- Centransdale High School
    o *At the corner of Centransdale High School (right end of building)... you can turn left to get to Westick Blvd. There's an alley next to a convenience store.*
    o *At the same corner of Centransdale High School... you can turn right to get to Venue Ave. If you continue walking straight, you'll reach Cuues Marketplace.*
    o *At Centransdale High School (in between the left end and right end of the building), if you exit out of the side doors and turn right, you'll be walking away from the school (your back is now facing the school as you're walking away from it). Continue walking away from the school and you're approaching Blake Street. Continue walking straight down this street to NH Pharmacy. Continue walking, you'll pass NH Pharmacy. The next street is Valmar Street (approx. 100 steps). You're walking one hundred more steps to Florestses street. There are many shopping centers in the area.*

- Cenbaile Street *This Street cuts through Tarainound Street. It's near Remeliat Street.*
- Venue Avenue

- o   Cuues Marketplace
- Westick Boulevard
  - o   Convenience Store next to an alley
  - o   Centransdale High School
- Blake Street
  - o   Going towards NH Pharmacy
  - o   NH Pharmacy opened in the Fall of 2107.
- Valmar Street
  - o   Passing NH Pharmacy
  - o   Hidendale Defenders Police Headquarters. *Two floor office space, car storage garage.*
  - o   Italia Ricci's Italian Guardalian Restaurant. *Two blocks from Hidendale Defenders HQ.*
- Florestses Street
  - o   Many shopping centers in this area.
  - o   Ion Foods *Sells nutritional snacks and your regular grocery.*
- Himswelm Street
  - o   Going to Narthaniel Park District
  - o   Abigail's Home for Youths Foster Care is here
  - o   The corner before you reach the foster care is Qwinzale's Convenience Store
- Benjamin Weismans Boulevard *Position yourself at Kïyla Gerald's residence and from there, four blocks north from Jayla's home.*
- Remeliat Street *Intersects with Tarainound Street.*
- Tarainound Street *A main street and a really long one. This street is a one-straight shot to many restaurants, convenience stores, and many cities.*
- Drekal Park District *The closest park to Tarainound Street with many art pieces in the center of the park.*

- Narthaniel Park District *The closest park to Himswelm Street, with one walkway and a children's park.*
- Abigail's Home for Youths Foster Care *Located on Himswelm Street next to Narthaniel Park District.*
- Drenden Mountain *Located behind Hidendale Observatory.*
- Marquee Arcade *Located on Cimdal Avenue, a few blocks away from Tarainound Street. The only arcade in town, filled with a wide variety of video games, including virtual games, two-player games, and more*
- Teen Realm Media Center 'T-Realm' *A place for teens. It's located a block away from Cimdal Avenue. There's video games, fast food buffet, information counter server, free internet access, virtual televisions to watch all your favorite movies and shows.*
- Maxie's Bar & Grill *Located down the street from arcade.*
- Crumarus Hospital *Located west of Tarainound Street. The hospital is closer to*
- *Wayworth Bridge, leading to Ococo Town, Illinois.*
- HiiWell Beach *A wide beach where couples, families, and young adults come to enjoy their free schedules. There's clean waters thanks to Kale County's Newoluir's Lake that lies behind Stratum Oil Industries and MechaWaste in Dowers City, IL. Stratum Oil and MechaWaste helps to purify the water supply. Unfortunately, there's a few problems with the Diamond and Ore Okiewa Chemical factory. Sometimes, there's chemical leaks that are detected in the water's supply. There's a bit of a huge distance between. Once chemicals make contact with the small lake in Dowers City, it travels through the underwater tunnels and eventually make contact with the waters at this beach.*
- Aions Hospital

o   *This one huge hospital. There are many patient room spaces, several offices for all higher staff member, four recreational rooms for patient recovery, two family waiting room centers filled with many forms of entertainment and prayer pamphlets, and three information centers for the three entrance zones (Zone Alpha, Bravo, and Charlie) to the hospitals. There is no entry past the information centers unless all personnel show a form of identification. They're very strict on this policy.*

o   Room 2118, Hall E *Mr. Maxill stayed inside this room. Wealthy members stay here.*

Kale County, Illinois *Fifteen minutes south of Hidendale Springs, IL.*

-   Kris Helmsdale Recreational hall
-   NH Pharmacy *A smaller pharmacy compared to the others.*
-   Miss Missy's Daycare *Located on Mitchel Street.*
-   Governor Stephan Gunneim's place of birth
-   Ion Foods *Sells nutritional snacks and your regular grocery. Ten minutes near Mitchel Street. Located on Rodabagel Avenue.*
-   Iron Row Apartment Complex
-   SpeedWay Rail Lines *A smaller and miniature sized train station. There's only two train services in and out of this area.*
-   Stratum Oil Industries *Third office location.*
-   Newoluir's Lake *lies behind Stratum Oil Industries*
-   McVanders Crafts N' Supplies, INC. *Abandoned since 2089.*
-   Pyro and Dyro's mother's home, Mrs. Amelia Daggerton. *On Rouche Street*

- Derick Jackson's home. *On Nathom Street, down from Iron Row Apartment Complex.*

Dowers City, Illinois *thirty minutes south of Hidendale Springs, IL.*

- VICE Secret Warehouse *This is where unnamed VICE scientists constructed many electronic emitters and the place DiLusion destroyed.*
- MechaWaste *A garbage waste and recycling separating facility.*
- Chainberland's coffeehouse *Located on Quail Street.*
- Dale's Shopping Center *Located on Quail Street, down from 43rd street, turn left.*
    - o VicLow *A designer shoe store.*
    - o DQ's Deluxe Grocery
    - o Kang's *A fashionable, gothic and emo style clothing store.*
    - o Lu's *An expensive female clothing store. Sell dresses and stylish leggings.*
    - o Pens-R *A store selling a variety of different kinds of pens.*
    - o CinAEma *A two-room theatre. Shows current and old-school movies.*
    - o Dac 'O Noodles *A Japanese and Swedish combo restaurant.*
    - o Burger Junior *A fast food hangout spot for young adults. Sells Kids Meal's,*
    - o *including a burger, French fries, soda and or milkshakes.*
    - o Icy Sam's *A frozen yogurt spot.*
    - o R Ams GO *Sells a variety of designer shoes. No dress shoes.*

- o Men's Style~House *A variety of business suits, including dress shoes.*
- o Click-Clack Toys *Sells many different and noisy children's toys.*
- o Ani<>More *A teen chill spot. Has toys, barbies plus action figures, and video*

- o *games to sell. The public can also view the televisions, displaying commercials of the newest items soon to be on sale at the store.*

- Diamond and Ore Okiewa Chemical Factory *located in the little forest of Dowers City*
  - o There's an unnamed lake right behind this factory. It's small but under the water there's underwater tunnels connecting to Newoluir's Lake in Kale County and HiiWell Beach in Hidendale Springs, IL.
- Q National Bank *Located on 44th & Pulaski Avenue.*
- NH Pharmacy+ *A store and there's a kiosk across from it.*
- Iron Steam Factory *The employees help create reinforced iron steel for building. This is on Quail Street. This building has been repaired in the beginning of the year 2098.*

Flavrare County (Town), Illinois *fifteen minutes north of Valousse City, IL.*

- One of Kelo Ritz's homes and one of his secret laboratories *Located on Gravers Street.*
- Mackie's Donuts Store
- NH Pharmacy *A smaller pharmacy store, compared to the others.*

- Gowdon's Prison *This place houses many inmates for all sorts of crimes.*
- Lexus Street *It's near a wide, open field, just down from Mackie's Donuts Store.*
- Iris's Fashion Jewelry Store
- Ion Foods *Sells nutritional snacks and your regular grocery. 30 minutes away from Gravers Street. Located on Noturor Street.*
- SpeedWay Rail Lines *SpeedWay Rail Train going in and out of the town.*
- Vickie Male's Play Park and Art Street *A children's playground and many pathways where lots of artwork are displayed.*

Valousse City, Illinois *thirty minutes south of Dowers City, IL.*

- Lincoln Oaks Mall *A huge shopping center with great but mostly expensive stores and a very few affordable ones.*
- NH Pharmacy
    o *A larger pharmacy. The largest one compared to the others in nearby cities. There is a plaque on the wall when you walk inside. It is the CEO, Neal Heartman. Mr. Heartman was involved in a tragic accident that cost him his life. This man dedicated his life to discovering a cure for cancer.*
- Anaheim Industries: Applied Sciences Division *Curtis Jemore Anaheim, owner and CEO*
- Lorisdale National Park *This park has trails lined with art sculptures, a center fountain, a children's playground, and a 3D walk-in house*
- Stratum Oil Industries *The Company's second office location.*

- Valora Docks *A docking port for fisherman with two warehouses for housing boats.*
- First National Bank
- InQuiZiehion
    - o *A local newsprint and media organization, also deals with online web content. Stan Bough is the editor-in-chief. This place is a tall building located on the west side of the city, at the corner of Seventh Street and Fifer Lane. The building's most distinguishing and famous feature is the enormous silver scroll sitting at an angle on top of the building.*
- Marwolon *A huge men's and women's department store.*
- Starwoks Coffee House
- Valousse Convention Center
- SpeedWay Rail Stations *SpeedWay Rail Trains going in and out of the city.*
- TechStrumm Industries *At the start of the New Year, a project was pushed forward. A sign is placed in front of the old building in January 2108 reading, "Coming Soon! Vale Corp-Industries"*
- R.Stop Tavern *Nowhere near the city. Three miles going southeast away from the city.*
- Ion Foods *Sells nutritional snacks and your regular grocery. 30 minutes from the Lincoln Oaks Mall. Located on Himole Street.*

Laroouse City, Illinois *An hour and thirty minutes west of Valousse City, IL.*

- Skyyas Airport

- SpeedWay Rail Stations *SpeedWay Rail Trains and GoRail Alpha Line, Bravo Line, and Charlie Line trains come in and out of this city from others faraway cities.*
- Nicolás el alimento *Spanish restaurant with many delicious foods. Located on Dekonkae Avenue.*
- Cromane Street *Walking away from Nicolás el alimento's Spanish restaurant.*
- Anqua Industries *An organization that finds new ways for living a comfortable life. There are many departments.*
  - o *Ewellon Department is the nation's leading competitive energy provider. The Anqua team and Ewellon staff participate in every stage of the energy business, from generation to competitive energy sales to transmission to delivery. Ewellon alone works in finding new ways to distribute electricity to various places, businesses, and residences. The president of this department, Tom Ewelling, is the creator of ELiPiP. A small device (no bigger than your average cell phone). This is a new unlimited power source that many businesses desire to have in their possession. It's clean, renewable energy. This device can receive and generate massive amounts of electricity within the programmed area.*
- Adlum Corporation
  - o *An organization that sponsors high-level corporate level campaigns. They work to support other growing companies, ensuring the best for the buck!*
- Starwoks Coffee House
- DOMs Arcade *This is the place where video game players, from all over the country, come to challenge each other for top prizes!*
- Emptied Meat Factory. *There's nothing here. It's abandoned*

Methphodollous Island *Located somewhere close off the East Coast of the United States*

- Primous Facility *A facility that houses psychotic individuals who have had mental breakdowns, hardened criminals, and the like; there is also talk of the facility being used to hold cross-humans*
- Security Station *VLORs personnel authorizes access to the gates of Primous.*

Naphilia Town, Illinois *Forty minutes east of Hidendale Springs, IL.*

- o A quiet suburbs. There is not much here. This is a just residential neighborhood.
- SpeedWay Rail Lines *SpeedWay Rail Train going in and out of the town.*
- Sysis June Lake *The beach where DiLuAH's ship crashed at night.*
- Clifaran Mountains *Ciemere Peak is the highest point and located on the center mountain.*
- E.X. PLODES Amusement Park *This ginormous theme park is currently being built. Projected time to be completed is sometime in the year 2108.*
- Fall Lake Retirement Home *Senior citizens over the age 70 are welcome.*
- Lake Meadows Apartments *Six floors of 3 bedroom spaces with one bathroom, one kitchen space, and a living area. Garages are in a separate building right next door to the property.*
- Ion Foods *Sells nutritional snacks and your regular grocery.*

Marina Bayou Harbor, Illinois

  o *Head south down Tarainound street. Three hours away from Hidendale Springs, Illinois.*

- Nelskex Park
- Starwoks Coffee House
- Construction Site: 'NEW! Suites Ft. Starwoks Coffee House' *Counchone Street.*
- A shipyard *Filled with tons of small fishing boats.*

Ococo Town, Illinois

  o *Drive on Wayworth Bridge to enter this town. The town is west of Tarainound Street, leaving Hidendale Springs, Illinois.*

- VeVideer Forest *A huge forest twenty miles from Hidendale Springs, Illinois.*
- Dokomo Park
- Starwoks Coffee House
- Casavol Beach *These are open waters (ships are free to pass through but not stop unless they're a small boat. The two piers are small. Civilians are welcome to enjoy their free time here with their families and loved ones. There's a few beach-styled restaurants near the waters.*
- Abandoned Warehouse *fifteen minutes away from VeVideer Forest*
- Old Carsodova Mansion. *This home is in pretty good condition. There's vines covering the entire house and stretching through the front yard garden that has grown expeditiously wild in under ten years being unoccupied.*
- Courtyard Gardens. *One Street west from the Carsodova Residence, lies the deceased family's former yard where they hosted many special occasions, including Bar Mitzvah ceremonies.*

- Courtyard Guard House. *Center of the Courtyard Gardens and behind lies old sewer systems leading to Gyrasion Providence, Gradelia City, and stretching farther out to even more exclusive cities and states far away. This was used long ago by founding families, but nowadays there's plants surrounding the area and no one living today knows about it.*

Gyrasion Providence, Illinois *Two hours and thirty minutes west of Tarainound Street*

- A seaport allowing U.S. Navy ships to dock because a base is located in the area.
- Medayo Drive *There are ten really huge houses. The wealthy lives here. Five bedrooms, three bathrooms, two kitchens spaces, a living area, and a dining area. There are garages attached to each house.*

Winndow City, Illinois

  o *A small city located right outside of Gyrasion Providence, Illinois. Two hours and forty minutes south of Tarainound Street.*
- Winnix Airlines *A small airport. There are a few airplanes that come to this airport.*
- Kaydale Hospital
- Starwoks Coffee House
- Mars Millennium Apartments *Located on Vonrou Street.*
- Ion Foods *Sells nutritional snacks and your regular grocery. Located on the worse part of town. On the verge of being shut down due to low numbers.*

Gradelia City, Illinois

- o *This city was built in the year 2019. This city became a major tourist attraction after the year 2030. There are many different restaurants, from every culture in the world.*
- NH Pharmacy
- Balibai Street
  - o Sushi Round'Omore
  - o Arrow Left → Tavern
  - o Ion Foods *Sells nutritional snacks and your regular grocery.*

Melaro Village, Indiana

- Juvenile Detention Center
- Starwoks Coffee House
- NH Pharmacy
- Ion Foods *Sells nutritional snacks and your regular grocery.*

Cauitry Town, Michigan *A very quiet town to live. The crime rate is down to zero percent.*

- Meliftorra Docks
- Crescent Boulevard *There are twenty townhomes, lined on both sides of the street.*
- Velneo Street
- Delrio Matte Grocery
  - o *At the end of Crescent Blvd, you'll get to Velneo Street. You'll have to turn left or right because it cuts through.*
- Starwoks Coffee House
- Delmont's Bank

Lamont Town, Michigan *One hour and forty minutes north of Hidendale Springs, IL.*

- Teekee Forest *A huge forest. There is nothing but trees.*
- Starwoks Coffee House
- NH Pharmacy
- Ion Foods *Sells nutritional snacks and your regular grocery.*

Falarbor Bay, Montana *A quiet place to live. There's a lot of boats and many fisherman.*

- Bayside Park *A children's park. Many themed fish slides and swing sets.*

Floraston, Montana *A lovely little town. A very nice place to live.*

- Moravale National Park *There's a tall building in front of it.*

Lake County, Montana *A moderately-sized city. A business area.*

- Lake County
- Polson Airport
- Ion Foods *Sells nutritional snacks and your regular grocery.*

Valey Sray, Colorado

- o *A huge valley of empty unused lands. There are no cattle or animals here. The*
- o *land is occupied with nothing but palm trees that are spaced twenty feet away from each other. About twenty yards out, there is nothing but grass and the mountains lie past there.*

- Boosechaimou
- MieLiMeiLi Desert *This place resembles a large desert but it's just a huge crater-sized hole in the ground. There is nothing near this place, no stores, etc.*

College Station, Texas *A city in East Central Texas in the heart of the Brazos Valley.*

- SpeedWay Rail Stations *A station where multiple trains leave and enter from different cities and states around the world and the station, with tracks, connecting to Melova-Metro Train Station in Melovaton City, South Carolina*
- Stratum Oil Industries *Main Office Location*
- Stratum Oil Employees Parking Garage *Outside near Stratum Oil Industry's Main Office Building*
- Starwoks Coffee House
- NH Pharmacy

Port Aransas, Texas *A city in Nueces County, TX*

- Stratum Oil Industries *Fourth built location*
- Stratum Oil Conference Hall *Location across the street from the main office building on Duole Street.*
- Tektons Shipyard
  - o Dozens of boats are stored.
- Marc's Warehouse *This place has been deserted for years. This place is undergoing a foreclosure (starting in the year 2042) that has yet to be settled.*

Arnesto Capital, Texas *Island on southern Texas border, points to Baton Rouge, LA*

- NH Pharmacy

Varilin Capitol, New York *A new, small island city sixty minutes from New York City*

- NH Pharmacy
- Tipalerdale Manor
    - o *A wealthy mistress lived and owned this home (been in her family for generations) before she died, leaving the house to an Asian immigrant turned successful businessman, in a few short years. The businessman is a Mr. Cinah Nyani Eroüsaki. The man built many accessories to the home but there's some additions that are a mystery to the public.*
- Starwoks Coffee House
- Jake's Donuts Shop

Chribale Isle *A newly but small, secluded island near Sandulay Island. There's only a forest here.*

- An unnamed and uninhabited forest turned into SciQui's personal prison.

Merritt Island, Florida *Twenty minutes from Vinrail County, FL. via the Merry-Jorry Ferry.*

- NalVa Space Station: Ground Unit
- Mariberea Harbor Ferry Port *Take a ride on the Merry-Jorry Ferry*

Vantlonon City, Florida

- Toxic Waste Dump
- Transportation Express Bus Center
- Starwoks Coffee House

- Ion Foods *Sells nutritional snacks and your regular grocery.*
- Ever Wanderah Flower Fields
    - o *This is the main attraction to the city. A city filled with many different kinds of beautiful and exotic looking flowers.*

Lorelaville, Florida *Forty minutes away from Lake City, Florida*

- NH Pharmacy
- Nieu Springs Central *A middle class neighborhood with many houses and apartments. This place in on Babalou Avenue.*
- Starwoks Coffee House
- Babalou Avenue connects to Calamaz Street.

Vinrail County, Florida *A small railroad town. Few civilians living here.*

- SpeedWay Rail Lines *SpeedWay Rail Train going in and out of the town.*
- NH Pharmacy

Fuuluchi Capitol, South Dakota

    - o *An island city similar to New York but much smaller and more suburban. The city is media-based, everyone has some kind of talent… whether musical, art, etc. Everyone who is born and raised here has high hopes to making it big and traveling to Hollywood Vale one day to seek out their dreams. Hollywood Vale is located on Sandulay Island.*

- Melanie's Dance Theatre for Performance Arts

- NH Pharmacy
- Starwoks Coffee House
- Ion Foods *Sells nutritional snacks and your regular grocery.*
- Dwelco's Pharmaceuticals
  - o *The pharmaceutical industry develops, produces, and markets drugs or pharmaceuticals for use as medications. Pharmaceutical companies may deal in generic or brand medications and medical devices. They are subject to a variety of laws and regulations that govern the patenting, testing, safety, efficacy and marketing of drugs.*

- Fuller Street
  - o Saint Frances de Lou Public High School
    - ▪ *The school is on Fuller Street, but he has to cross railroad tracks to get to the school. The tracks lead toward a bridge going directly over water to the next town. Rithmul Street is where he actually lives. The streets cross each other. Fuller Street is longer. The school is a straight shot from Rhin's house, approximately about twenty minutes away and the tracks is where the separation lie.*
- Rithmul Street
  - o *A secondary Street Rhin's house lies on besides saying Fuller Street.*
- Nthorow Avenue
  - o Leads to Aorthordocee Bridge
    - ▪ *Takes you off the island and to the mainland of South Dakota.*
- McGregor's Street
  - o *Intersects Fuller Street, leading to the local school, Saint Frances de Lou High School, and the*

shopping center. Mr. Bhim Phantolok's place of residence is located here.

- MiiChi's Vir-Cade
    - o *A virtual arcade with more virtual reality games, including 3D augmented reality games.*
- RaisDale Plaza
    - o RaisDale Cinema
    - o Norisa's Hair and Makeup Salon
    - o Chuck's Barbershop
    - o T&N's Shoe Tailor
    - o Starwoks Coffee House
    - o VicLow *A designer shoe store.*
    - o Chip N' Curry *Japanese cuisine.*
    - o New-World Center Stage *Center Plaza, shows off new talents.*
    - o Mitch & Mike's Emporium
    - o Jack Burgers N' Aimee's Hotdogs
    - o J&J Grocery
    - o Skate O' Skate Rink Rail *A huge roller skating rink with rails used by extreme daredevils and large ramps for experienced skateboarders and bikers.*

HighTech City, Georgia

- Home to the HTQ Police Force
    - o **HighTech City HQ Police Force** --- lies in the center of HighTech City, GA. The police force have orders, from Captain Sky Duebron, to protect the city and nearby towns. The whole operation is run by the Captain. The people under him are his officers, his operators, his detectives and

his Junior Squad Division also referred to as the In-Training Division.

- GeoComm Enterprises *Second Built Location*
- Dutanburg Trail Park
- Techy Mountains
- Downtown Bus and Ship Port Station
- HighTech Central Plaza has a Memorial Fountain and a Statue of the Founder
    - o *The founder, Damone Allikust, is a war hero who gave his life to many Americans. He was a General in the U.S. Army. He moved on to serve as the first Commander at HighTech City's Police Force. He was the one who got a bill passed to start a youth training department, the JSD (Junior Squad Division), in order to train new soldiers and police officers. His focus was to help inner city children gain skills that will help make them excellent leaders. As a young man, he fought in a mystery war against the Jolt'Tweillers and the Shoc'Weillers. The President of the United States, at the time, kept this a secret from the public… that and a VLORICE agent got involved. BORN: October 20th 1987 - DIED: June 6th 2064*
- Information & Travel Building
- Editorial Office is located inside. *This is a small news and media firm. It doesn't do too well now that the Inquiziehion is growing ever so popular around the world.*
- Hii'Est Beach *Beautiful but has a few minor annoyances*
- Hii'Est Beach Café
- Hii-Est Pier *Near Tech-Trail Forest*
- Starwoks Coffee Mini-House
- Ion Foods *Sells nutritional snacks and your regular grocery.*
- Tech-Trail Forest

- HighTech Bridge *connecting to Curross Town*
- Transportation Express Bus Center
- HighTech University

Niechest Town, Georgia *The town is known as a flourishing Garden City. The town's growing every day.*

  o *Border of HighTech City, north of Techy Mountains*
- Madam Urathane Alma's cottage is in Techy Mountain area.
- Neirolo Cavern. *An inter-dimensional gateway to the multi-worlds. This place has Transporter Relics inside the cave, buried under rubble. It wasn't intentional.*
- NH Medical Clinic
- Cheesar Forest with a Melody Lake
- M'Burgers 'n Shakes
- Starwoks Coffee House
- M'Burgers 'n Shakes *Opened March 2107*
- Mec's Family Bar & Tavern
  o *There's a small garden outside.*
- *le Restaurant*
- *le Cafe et tu*

Curross Town, Georgia

  o Border of HighTech City, south of Techy Mountains
- Medical Facility for Psychiatric Help

NieCross City, North Carolina

- NiLum Facility Jail
- NH Pharmacy

Atlanta, Georgia

- Fish Market

Melovaton City, South Carolina.

> o *There are three entrances into this city. When Melova Desert ends, you'll enter the city's southern gate. When heading out of Meadowy Way, you'll be leaving out the northern gate. The last remaining entrance is in front of NickelsFront Mall. This is the east gate. The east gate is between the other two entrances, left side once entering Melovaton City. Melova Square is the center of the city where the flamboyant mayor hosts events in the city. Melova Square is in front of the east gate and behind Melova Square is NickelsFront Mall.*

- Melova Desert *The only way into the city. The South Gate is located here.*
- GeoComm Enterprises *The Main Office. There are only two in the United States.*
- Sysmosis Shopping Center *Groceries, Clothing, Everyday items & more*
- MelFlora's Talent Stage *A small, circle stage in the center of the city. Tourist Attraction.*
- Starwoks Coffee House
- Medical Facility: Psychiatric Help
- Melova-Metro Train Station *Ride anywhere in the United States.*
- Vale Industries-Corp: TRI Communications Department *Two locations in the U.S.*

- Meadowy Way *Way out of the city, located by West gate. Continue walking to Cattesulby Woods.*
- Cattesulby Woods. *Keep walking you get closer to Eximpplest Town, SC.*
- NickelsFront Mall *The East Gate.*
- Melova Square.

Eximpplest Town, South Carolina.

- Catsugue Forest *This forest is connected to Cattesulby Woods.*

Great Similiete, Nevada.

- Fort Oxnile
    o Naval Spec Ops Command Training Facility *Jayn's last duty station.*

In the year 2020, California broke into three new peninsulas, which drifted from California's original position. **Oirailie Island** is a new island that drifted north and is now the Northern California Peninsula. Oirailie Island's eastern beach points toward Washington State. **Sandulay Island** is the second newest island, which drifted west and is far off on its own. **Qudruewley Island** is the third newest island. It drifted southeast. The three new California peninsulas, all large islands, each have a Northern Beach, an Eastern Beach, a Southern Beach, and a Western Beach.

Oirailie Island

- Northern Beach *This beach is unkempt and dirty in the year 2107. It's been this way for a while. A hidden laboratory was discovered, after exploding, in the year 2082.*
- Eastern Beach
- Western Beach
- Southern Beach

Sandulay Island

- o *The city of San Francisco is here with little to no change as in the year 2007.*
- San Drean
  - o NH Pharmacy
  - o Pellious Medical Clinic
  - o Angelica's Rare Finds Shop
  - o Starwoks Coffee House
  - o T&N Convenience Mart
  - o Hollywood Vale *Quite similar to the old and a more evolved Hollywood*
  - o FropYoli Shop *This place is a local ice cream shop.*
- Northern Beach
- Eastern Beach
- Western Beach *This area is nothing but ruins of old destroyed buildings. Due to the destruction of the old Golden Gate Bridge, this island became lost to the California Peninsulas. There may or may not be humans who live here. There's a place where plants and vegetation grows, but this island is mostly uninhabited.*
  - o Cremmosis Street
    - ▪ *An abandoned convenience store boarded up with steel plates with metallic bolts.*
  - o Delloris Avenue

o   Ruins of the old Golden Gate Bridge
-    Southern Beach

Qudruewley Island

o   *The two cities, Los Angeles and San Diego, are
still very much the same as in the year 2007.*
-    Northern Beach
-    Eastern Beach
-    Western Beach
-    Southern Beach

To get to Marina Bayou Harbor, Illinois...

Head south down Tarainound Street... Yeah! That long
street. It is exactly three hours away from Hidendale Springs,
Illinois. (If you are walking on foot.)

Miryova Price's Residence

She lives with her daughter, Jayla Price. The two live three
blocks down the street from Zadarion's home. Miryova rents
a space in the apartment building, near a suburban area.

The suburban area is a residential area existing commuting
distance to the main street, Tarainound Street.

The building is painted a dark orange color, with white
horizontal lines painted on building. The building is much
larger than Zadarion's home. His home is a two-story house.

At Miryova's residence, there's an entrance in the front and
through the left side of the building (facing from the street).

There is one back entrance as well, leading to Miryova's handmade garden. She talked to the landlord about building a garden. Miryova grows distinguished and exotic flowers that are out of this world! They would make you believe you're living in Paris, France and various other locations. There is a minimum number of African Americans living on her block, Cenbaile Street.

New Waii Island is a small island located somewhere in the Atlantic Ocean. At the end of the twenty-first century (2095) an island lifted from under water in the middle of the Atlantic Ocean, right across somewhere near the south part of South America. A few people from all over the world flocked to and inhabited this new island. The island became overpopulated within a few short months. The island is believed to be the lost city of Atlantis that disappeared a long time ago. A few nonbelievers that say this is a fairy tale. The people of the new island are referred to as, Atlantis Dwellers. Within a year, a city was built. Still the only city on the island, it is called **New Waii City**.

Mount Caubvick is a mountain located near Labrador and Quebec. This is in the Selamiut Range of the Torngat Mountains. In 2015, Mount Caubvick was one of the highest points in mainland Canada east of Alberta).

Detroit-Windsor Tunnel was the fourth international border crossing between Michigan and Canada. This was not built as a bridge, but as an underground tunnel. It connects the Interstate of 75 in Detroit with Highway 401 in Windsor, the tunnel opened in 1930. In 2107, no vehicle has permission to cross this old international underwater crossing. The tunnel collapsed in the year 2040, creating a gorge.

Moose Mountain is a peak in the Sawtooth Mountains of northeastern Minnesota in the United States. The elevation dropped few feet (1689 feet (515 meters) in the year 2017 and currently 1574 feet) above sea level. This area is located close to Lake Superior and reaching 1087 feet above its waters.

Quad Cities. Around the compound of cities, at the Iowa-Illinois border, near the Mississippi River, this area includes three main towns... Rocky Pavilion (used to be known as, Rock Island), Central Moline (used to be called, Moline and East Moline but now one), Davenport, and Little Bettendorf, Iowa. These are adjacent communities.

In the year, 2045, Little Bettendorf, and the closer communities, went through many tragic earthquakes occurring in Illinois starting May 16, 2045. The shock which knocked over many brick-made chimneys at Moline (now Central Moline) was felt over 550,000 square miles and strongly felt in Iowa, Wisconsin, and a little bit in certain parts of Michigan. Buildings swayed in Chicago, but microscopic near this city. There was fear that the walls near the city's dams would collapse, but nothing too tragic happened.

Two months later and a second intensity VII earthquake struck on July 22, 2045, knocking down brick-made chimneys in Davenport, Illinois, and in Central Moline, and Bettendorf, Iowa. Over forty windows were destroyed, bricks loosened, and plaster cracked in the Moline area. It was felt over only 32,425 square miles.

On August 03, 2045, a sharp but local shock occurred at Vicpol, a small and quiet town of about 250 people. The magnitude three shocks broke chimneys, cracked walls, knocked groceries from the shelves, and contaminated the water supply. Thunderous earth noises were heard. It was felt throughout the Quad Cities, and all towns less than ten miles away (these other cities suffered little changes). Six aftershocks were felt. It is thought-provoking to correlate this shock with the May 26, 1909, shock and the 1968 shock (all had maximum intensities of VII, but two had distinctively large feet areas more than 250 times greater than that of the Tamms earthquake).

These earthquakes changed these towns forever. Molina became a barren wasteland.

Fifty years later, the year 2095, a Spanish drug lord, Aleixo Ricardo Adoración, brought tyranny to the area.

Despite it being uninhabited, Adoración, brought all kinds of people to this area. They were underground slaves, so no one knew about them. These people were on LOST & FOUND lists posted in almost every grocery store; a few from the United States and many from Spanish countries.

Sometime after VLORICE split into two separate organizations, the former VLORs commander sent an agent to bring an end to Adoración's reign. After that, the people there were free to live in peace. Many businesses were started, and everyone lived as merchants, selling to make a living with the goods they either found or made by hand. The United States Government wanted to help these people financially, but someone deep in connections with the president and House of Representatives somehow made them forget about the people in Moline. This place, currently, resembles Mexico in the year 2015.

VICE Basement *An unknown room where Scientist Mario Vega does his secret experiments and invents new technology. Mario Vega never sees the light of day.*

APPENDIX 2

VLORs & VICE TECHNOLOGY, EQUIPMENT, AND GEAR

The V-Link *(see photo at the end of Book one)* is a high-tech digital watch that combines with the user's central nervous system. It transforms the civilian into his or her agent gear, is used to summon artillery and weapons, can teleport the agent, and is activated by the agent's thoughts and physical movements. Its features include:

- **Headset**. *The V-Link headset is worn on the forehead and used to communicate with people who are also wearing one*
- **V-Cuffs**. *A small, round, slick piece of metal that opens into a spiral and binds around an enemy to immobilize the person.*
- **Invisi-Dome**. *A circular barrier used to cover an area of a city or town, which cannot be seen by normal civilians and also prevents them from seeing what is happening inside the barrier. These keep civilians safe and prevent foes from escaping. Any VLORs member with a V-Link can enter a dome. Once activated, a dome affects all technology in the area, and any normal civilian inside one will have his or her memory of the experience automatically erased. Invisi-Domes also have restoring properties to fix property damage.*
- **Tiny Grenade Pellets**. *Exploding bombs that don't do heavy damage.*
- **Flame Igniter**. *Resembles a pocket lighter, but thin and long. It produces quick flame.*

- **Deflector Shield**. *A near invisible shield. Once activated, it's in the shape of a circle. Able to see through it and nothing can get through.*

- **Gasoline Capsules**. *A capsule that contains gasoline inside it.*

- **Holo-Messages**. *3D telephone calls.*

- **Q3 Explosives**. *Small devices that send sonic screeches to clear away particles such as dirt, small rocks, and the like.*

- **Q6 Explosives**. *Medium-sized devices that sends sonic screeches to clear away heavier material.*

- **Q9 Explosives**. *Small, cubed devices that expand and send sonic screeches that can destroy everything within a one-mile radius.*

- **Scope Lens**. *A tool that gives the agent the ability to see through walls.*

- **Tiny Daggers**. *Tiny swords for throwing at your opponent, used only by Agent Rahz.*

- **Tracker.** *A small disk, about the size of an American dime that, when attached to anything, allows the user to follow an individual.*

- **BIO-Beings.** *A new technology, not revealed until VLORs & VICE VOLUME II, was manufactured using Anaheim's technology. They are digital human bodies made to engage in missions as part of a project that was terminated after Curdur (an evil inside Agent Z) was born.*

- **V-Inducer**. *A small object that, when thrown, closes around an object or a physical being. Once trapped, whatever is inside the V-Inducer is destroyed by a blaze of fire. Nothing can resist the intense flames a V-Inducer can produce.*

- **V-Veil**. *A small, dime-sized coin. Once attached to a person, it turns them invisible. If the person is unconscious, they will remain that way as long as the device is in place.*

- **V-Haler**. *The V-Haler is a protective body suit, equipped to protect agents from terrible flames.*
- **V-Shield**. *An invisible shield that covers an individual, shielding them from bodily harm.*
- **V-Copier**. *This is a built-in function. It can produce multiple copies of anything, tangible or intangible. Although, the copies are like intangible objects.*
- **V-Absorber**. *This is a see-through thin blanket. Once it materializes and a person throws it, the very thin blanket unfolds and surrounds any kind of small particles such as… sleet, hail, sand, dust, etc.*
- **V-Line.** *A very thin and strong rope.*
- **TripCoin.** *Can change its weight.*
- **V-Cushioner.** *A small object, inside of a capsule. Once a person lets go of it, it can increase in weight. This causes it to weigh roughly about five hundred tons. It can later turn into a large seat cushion to soften a fall.*
- **V-PoLi.** *A function in the V-Link. A general purpose lie detector test, enabling VLORs to uncover hidden truths. This function embedded into the V-Link, once attached to a body, can read a person's mind. It uncovers what's fact and / or deceptive.*
- **V-Medical Supply Kit.** *Primary medical equipment used in the field. This kit is connected to VLORs HQ's medical center database. The VLORs medical center has many items.*
- **Silent Dyber.** *A small device capable of blocking out all forms of noises and communication, including speaking and breathing, for miles.*
- **V-MeMinifiers.** *These are small earpiece devices that materialize into an individual's ear to block out annoying noises at high frequencies. These small devices work very well.*

APPENDIX 3

NEW TECHNOLOGY

Creator… Scientist Rayley Nickolson

- **Scanner Satellite**. *A main satellite in outer space. It is cloaked and not easily detected. This is now separate from VICE. VICE is in the works of attaining their own. The V-Link connects to this satellite as well as VLORs's personal satellite that is attached to their base of operations… wherever VLORs HQ is located.*
- **Vactra Boots**. *Footwear with built-in gliding and rocket devices that enables agents to go airborne or to skate two inches off the ground.*
- **Vactra Flight Board**. *A glider that materializes from Z's V-Link and Agent Z's mode of transport.*
- **Vactra Sword**. *Agent Z's first sword. He is still a novice swordsman while using.*
- **Vactra Cutters**. *Lower left and right arm blades that eject from devices on the agent's wrists and Agent Caj's main weapon.*
- **Vactra Daggers**. *Sharp twin blades and Agent Rahz's main weapon.*
- **Vactra Blasters**. *A blaster every agent is equipped with. Emits a laser blast.*
- **Vactra Armor**. *In progress of being perfected. Arm extender with blaster. A metallic band that can expand, making an arm blaster. In the near future will be able to become a suit of armor.*
- **Vactra Bubbles**. *Transparent bubble traps.*

- **Vactra Boppers**. *Boxing gloves that pack a devastating, dynamic punch.*
- **Vactra Cycle**. *Operator Agent Rev. Travels through rough seas.*
- **Taser-Blades.** *These resemble regular Taser's but they're like daggers.*

Weapons Origin from… Unknown and now disbanded clan of Japanese warriors.

- **Shibarion Blade**. *Agent Z's re-designed sword. His main weapon of choice.*
- **Shibarion Blade-Blaster**. *Agent CQua's main weapon. Able to manually change into a blaster or into a blade.*
- **Shibarion Swigger**. *A weapon that can change into a V-Tracer and a Whip-like lash (think of a lion tamer).*

APPENDIX 4

MYSTERIOUS AND MISCELLANEOUS OBJECTS

- **Repliara Crystatite**. *A rare crystal that copies a person's identity. If the imposter's appearance cracks, white lights expel out of the person who has taken another's appearance, returning that person to his or her normal self. The inventor is a mystery even to this day.*
- **The Flamethrower Unit**. *Built by Curtis Anaheim, The Fire Starter. Slightly resembles a normal MK-47 but it is much larger.*
- **SupeXoil**. *Capsules containing a viscous liquid derived from petroleum that can be used as a fuel or lubricant. The petroleum has been modified with an unknown substance. The scientist who created this technology is a mystery. This special oil was converted from crude oil to diesel fuel and then to an unknown chemical. It is used to power machines and only Stratum Oil Industries has access to it.*
- **SupeXelectric**. Capsules containing an electric substance used to power machines and created by Stratum Oil Industries.
- **Dale's QPad**. *A money transfer device used by Dale Jr. It is just an electronic keypad.*
- **ELiPiP**. *This small device (no bigger than your average cell phone) is a new unlimited power source that many businesses desire to have in their possession. It's clean, renewable energy. This device can receive and generate massive amounts of electricity within the programmed area.*
- **Silencer Stag**. *A thin needle-like twig-shaped object. If makes contact with the skin, one will pass out.*

- **T-04 Zero Memory Gas Spray**. *A spray that will wipe memories.*
- **Vex Armor Emblem**. *An item found by Agent Z and his little band of creature-friends during his time on planet Vexion.*
- **Opla Whistle.** *A normal looking whistle that can emit a silent sound capable of memory erasing.*
- **Paranormal Detection Reader, PDR**. *A device made by Louis Gravnelle. He built this unique device in order to pick up supernatural activity anywhere.*
- **The Cryo-Cap.** *A regular capsule with a coordinate codes panel embedded into the device. This can put a human in cryosleep (a state of suspended animation) and teleports individual to any location typed into its system.*

APPENDIX 5

1999

- Krarnaca crash lands on Earth.

2007

- This year marked the end of the Shoc'Weillers and the Jolt'Tweillers, a race of lightning warriors and a superior form of homosapiens. A secret government assault was ordered by the president of the United States on December 31, 2007. This mysterious race of people had to be extinguished because they were a danger to mankind, according to the United States Military. Guardian Gai was attacked. He was struck by the deadly attack, The Deat'Low. This powerful attack can immobilize a person and it infects them with a horrendous illness. He died on October 1, 2007. Tundarick was also killed that same day, protecting him because it was his main job.

2020

- California broke into three new peninsulas, which drifted from California's original position. The three new California peninsulas all have a Northern Beach, an Eastern Beach, a Southern Beach, and a Western Beach. All three peninsulas are huge and contain many cities.
- **Oirailie Island** is a new island that drifted north and became the Northern California Peninsula.

Oirailie Island's eastern beach points toward the state of Washington.

- **Sandulay Island** is a new island that drifted west, and is far off on its own. This is the Western California Peninsula.
- **Qudruewley Island** drifted southeast and became the Southern California Peninsula.
- A new island near the island of Japan was named, **Iitchii Mils** by the Japanese locals in the area. The Supreme Family, Wasaki, lives here and rules the island with their elite troops of ninja assassin warriors. Today, the Leader of the Wasaki family has stopped all actions on creating order in Japan and Korea. He sits and relaxes in his castle. In the future, he will have a few children who will be banished across the globe for their terrible natures. In the future, one of his children, the youngest, will be the only one left at the Wasaki home.

2030

- This year saw a marked rise in unemployment in the United States.
- Dale Falakar Sr. had four Stratum Oil facilities built in various places in the United States.

2068

- Madin Doro Torres was born.

2076

- Xavier Marshall was born

2079

- Tundarick was reborn.

2080

- A mysterious sheet of metal crashed on planet Earth. Naralina was born.

2082

- Samuel Marshall brought his six year old son Xavier to a secret lab on Northern Beach on Oirailie Island. The secret lab was destroyed.

2085

- DiLuAH's ship recovered from its malfunction in outer space, and his ship crashed on planet Earth near Sysis June Lake in Naphilia Town, Illinois. The ship exploded, and the passenger escaped. Miles away in Hidendale Springs, Illinois, where he had long been buried in a cave deep underneath the city, the cursed knight's tomb cracked open.

2088

- Xavier Marshall returned home with father after a long trip on their overseas adventure.

2089

- Xavier Marshall fell in love with beautiful girl. Drey (Sirus Langford) was born. Michel Johnson was born.

2090

- Jack McKoy was born. Ronald Osaida was born. Krarnaca, now known as Doc Krarn, was hired into VICE.
- June of this year, unemployment dropped 10 % in the United States.

2091

- Jodana Uvarla was born.

2092

- Jacque Baller was born. Joel Rodriquez was born. Lin Yiu Gustov was born. Gai Tunh Chi was reborn.

2093

- A war took place in the Namorant Dimension (Damonarian v. Quinoragoras). A few individuals, including Mayana's parents, arrived on Earth.
- Xavier Marshall collapsed and slipped into a coma. Rhin Kashioko was born. Jennifer Wayner was born.

2094

- Ryan (Zada) 'Z' Jones was born. Mhariah (Zari) 'Rahz' Johnson was born. Jayla Price was born. Kiyla Gerald was born. Alecxander 'Shocker' Jackson was born. Morgan Wiles was born.

2095

- A new island floated up somewhere in the Atlantic Ocean and was officially named New Waii Island. Rivi was born and later found on the island by elder Krojo. Valery Maxill was born.

2096

- Eraine 'Floral' Delpro've was born.

2098

- In the Namorant Dimension, the remaining Quinoragoras took refuge on planet Devina. They took over the Devion's home world. A young knight (Jaylin) was born. The mysterious cursed knight crawled out from under Drenden Mountain, located in Hidendale Springs, Illinois. The cursed knight explored this new world.

2100

- Mayana 'Maya' Johnson was born.

2102

- Young Alec was eight years old when he saw his mother's lifeless body dangling from a light pole on Sandulay Island.

2103

- Joel Rodriguez became a cross-human. He started calling himself, ShaVenger.

2105

- Dani discovered information about her uncle, Raymond Dilles, also known as, The Gallant Gamer. During the takeover of the twins' new virtual world, she uncovered the hacker's identity and what he's done in the past. A recent event mentioned why he was imprisoned at NiLum Prison and later released on good behavior in the year 2105.

2106

- Ki'liana (Kiley) Jones was born.

2107

- *Friday, June 9, 2107*, A Centransdale High School graduate, Morales Ewelling, stalks Mr. Anaheim and begs him to hire him.
- *Monday, June 12, 2107*, Donny and Sally knocks over Agent Z in Bayside Park. The park is located in Falarbor Bay, Montana.
- *Monday, June 12, 2107*, a young man, Agent Eron, is in the city of San Drean, located on Sandulay Island. He's enjoying one of his favorite treats inside FropYoli's Ice Cream Shop.
- *Tuesday, June 13, 2107*, Mitch and Rich are sentenced to do six months of community service and will begin their house arrest from June 13th 2107 to March 13th 2108.
- *Tuesday, June 13, 2107*, Unknown drunk driver who killed Brady Forbes and Michel Johnson will serve

twelve years at Gowdon's Prison. The penalty is six years, but there were two deaths.

- *Thursday, June 15, 2107,* Mr. Sturgess McMillan committed suicide. He refused to be taken into custody after Agent Caj brought an end to the terrorist organization known as ZEXTERN.

- *Sunday, June 18, 2107,* Mrs. Amelia Daggerton dies in her home on Rouche Street located in Kale County, Illinois.

- *Friday, August 04th, 2107,* A medium-sized odd-shaped stone fell out of a portal after DiLusion and Commander Xavier returned to Earth via the same portal.

- *Wednesday, September 13, 2107,* Agent Z battled a new guy after defeating and destroying a mysterious new robot in Valousse City. During the confrontation, he deduced that Eron was wearing a special suit close to the ones him and Rev wear as VLORs agents. He plans on finding out the identity of this newcomer.

- *Wednesday, September 13, 2107* – Agent Z went to SciQui's personal island home and asked him a series of questions pertaining to the mysterious armband and the Vex Armor Emblem. He seems to be satisfied with SciQui's responses.

- *Tuesday, January 01, 2108* – Reesa McCulkin is hired at the InquiZiehion.

APPENDIX 6

DIMENSIONS, PLANETS... NEW WORLDS THE NAMORANT DIMENSION

There are ten planets, surrounding one lone moon. One planet was moved.

Junio's Moon
- Guardian of Malithia Reign's Here
  - o The center of the Namorant Dimension and Pluto's *(The moon located in the Isolated Dimension.)* connecting twin.

Sol Moon
- Main Moon in the Namorant Dimension and it acts like the Sun does in the Isolated Dimension.

Devlerlue Moon
- This moon is closest to planet Devina. This moon only helps out planet Devina, providing energy and nutrients to plant life, etc.
- The time on planet Devina is based on the setting of the red and blue moon, the Devlerlue moon. The colors on this moon shift patterns, letting the Devions know when it's day out or night out. The sky remains dark. The sky never brightens.

Vrec Planet
- Home to the Vrecians
  - o A race of Homo Sapiens that live above the planets core.

- Home to the Damonarians, morphed Homo Sapiens that live on the surface of the planet.
  - Crayos Forest is an ancient forest. Inside the forest is a device capable to transport an individual to other worlds. Located on the planet's surface.

Vexion Planet
- Home to many different breeds of creatures
  - *PLACES*
    - Maranious Forest
    - Kilanene Valley
    - Keikien City
      - King Keikaie's Castle
    - Volsus Caverns
    - Moonz Valley
    - Kepler Forest
      - Forest of the Fallen
    - Vantronus Valley
    - The Dark Land, formerly an empty field of grass. This area is now corrupted by dark energy. Anything that touches this area is changed forever. There's no telling how they'll be changed… either genetically or mentally.

Coroth Planet
- Home to Homo Sapiens, very similar to Earth humans but their bodies are more sturdier.
  - i.e. Kokashi, Dreyke, DomiNix and Xhirsten's new home
  - *PLACES*

- Council of Coro
- Methordarion Temple
- Rapture Forest
- Coroth Pavilion is the home where everyone lives. The houses are built right beside each other.

Vaoth Planet

- Home to Homo Sapiens with a green-colored skin tone.
  - i.e. Chloe, Prince Warzen

  o *PLACES*
    - King's Temple *(current King is King Diyas Warzen II)*
    - Rullie Lands are three areas of nothing but tall trees. These are homes for creatures living on the planet.
    - Vaoth Pavilion is the home where everyone lives. The houses are built right beside each other.

Naoth Planet *(New Coroth)*

- Homeworld to Homo Sapiens, very similar to Earth humans but their bodies are more sturdier. This planet is new. People living on Coroth founded and inhabited this planet. A female (Nical Winterl) had a few people from planet Coroth transferred to a new inhabitable planet, planet Naoth. She became the Queen. The current queen is her granddaughter.

This planet is primarily ruled by females. The males that are born on this planet are sent to planet Coroth. It's like an exchange.

- i.e. Quarah and new home for Goriah

o *PLACES*

- Queen's Palace *(current Queen is Veriala Winterl)*
- Diesca Palias are two areas of nothing but tall trees. These are homes for creatures living on the planet.
- Naoth Pavilion is the home where everyone lives. The houses are built right beside each other.

Xirxion Planet

- Home to Xirxes Race.
  o This world is a waste land. A laser was fired from an unknown location via space portal and wiped out the entire species. They're all extinct. There is only one Xirxes child that lives.

Quidior Planet

- Home to Quinoragoras Creatures.
  o This world is a now a wasteland. A Great Devastating War (Quinoragoras v. Damonarians) is the cause. It was the battle ground where many races

(mostly Quinoragoras) lost their lives. An uninhabitable world.

Devina Planet

- Home to the Devions
    - o A very peaceful but a small race of creatures. There is a small population of them.
    - o *PLACES*
        - Camp Qui (Tecquine Lands)
            - Verrosl Stream is the only place to find water.
            - There are no hills or mountains in this area.
        - Quidior Capitol
            - Built in the middle of both camps in the middle of nowhere. A Quinoragoras tower where the revived King Gorvin spends most of his time.
        - Camp Nor (Deckaquine Lands)
            - There's a small amount of water, inside the only two mountains in this area. This area is a harsh environment. Many Devions try to avoid coming to this area. If a Devion hangs around here, they're most likely trouble.
            - Somewhere deep underground, very

close by, lies Dextorey's laboratory.

- Frezarden Top is a tall mountain. It's extremely very cold at the top.

Xeiar Planet

- Home to all-powerful Homo Sapiens
  - o They look like Earth humans but their bodies store endless amounts of magical energy (Xeiar Magic). i.e. Wizards, Witches, and Oracles. There are also many monstrous creatures. A few of them are similar to those from planet Vexion.
  - o This planet is now a great distance away from the other planets. A magical barrier prevents non-magical creatures from entering this world.
  - o *PLACES*
    - Gateway to Valdesmon World lies behind Grand Xesus.
    - Grand Xesus is a meeting place for the Great Xeiar Wizards.
    - Council Pavilax is a stage-like area where the guilty (for any crimes) are brought before the Great Xeiar Wizards. King Makliton granted authority for the three Great Wizards to deal with the wronged.
    - Xeitri Lands are four areas of nothing but tall trees. These trees surround Grand Xesus. There are

creatures, living on the planet, who make their home beyond this area. Xeiar wizards live anywhere they like. The majority of them live in-between Xeitri Lands and Grand Xesus.

- Xai Pav is the home where everyone lives. The houses are built right beside each other.
- McKelnor's Cliff
- Valley of Blist
- Los Xeiar is an area where the old kingdom burned down. What remains is nothing but old and torn down castle ruins. This area is a great distance away from Xeitri Lands.
- MaKahMer Volcano is a long way from Xeitri Lands. It's all the way on the other side of the planet. There are trees at the bottom of this volcano.
- Xanpo's Place is a small island near MaKahMer Volcano. It's a safe house.

Extiepenia Planet

- Home to homo-sapiens whose powers derive from supernatural and paranormal forces.
  - o i.e. Goriah's place of birth
  - o They resemble Earth humans but their eyes are monstrous. Their eyes are alien.

o   Deep underground lives powerful ghost creatures, Penialia's. Once awakened from slumber, they seek an Extiepian and makes them their host body. Penialia's are transparent creatures. Their bodies are ghostly.

THE ISOLATED DIMENSION

This dimension is believed to be the center of the universe.

Earth Planet

- Home to Homo Sapiens
    - o   i.e. Humans, many different species of animals, and lots of different plant life.

Vegues Planet

- o   2,000,000,000 Light years away from Earth
- Home to Morphenile Creatures with purple skin
    - o   i.e. DiLuAH and CoLesTro

Kao 95th Planet

- o   2,000,000,000 Light years away from Earth
- Home to Reptilian, many legged creatures
    - o   i.e. Doc Krarn

Vartan Planet

- o 2,000,000,000 Light years away from Earth
- Home to Block, stony mole-like creatures
  - o i.e. the former King Varnican

VALDESMON WORLD

The dark prison world is the ultimate prison used in the Namorant Dimension by the Great Wizards of Xeiar and other powerful entities. There were many creatures (aliens) imprisoned in this dark prison.

o **DARKEIL DIMENSION**

A dark hell. An afterlife where the former living call home.

Everyone living entity from the Namorant Dimension believes Darkeil is an afterlife for all former living entities. The former living spirits have no possibility of a return. There is a slight possibility that a living spirit may still be alive if sent Darkeil by mistake. Everyone from the Isolated Dimension (especially on planet Earth) call this, Hell.

VIRT WORLD

A special digital world created by Dani and Rani Darivele, using a gaming console from 1991 they found.

LOCATIONS

- Mill's Red Road. A long road (almost like Tarainound Street), connecting to many places. This is the one and only road in this digital world.

APPENDIX 7

XEIAR SPELLS

Ventis – *Summons a cloud of paralyzing / sleepiness / poison smoke*

Nieeth – *Summons a see-through shield*

Nieeth-Thro – *Flicks away any attack with the sweep of a hand*

Gorgantro – *Creates stone pillars around a target and traps the person*

Nozespro Cuulazostras – *A wizard's special attack in the form of a BlastBeam*

Nozespro Cuulazostras Zestras – *A BlastBeam with electricity around it*

Blitargo – *If enemy is close, they are immediately pushed away*

Lita – *Illuminates the entire area within a fifty foot radius*

Cofrea Camoses Tarar – *A mixture of colorful lights and a barrage of attacks*

Healoris – *Able to heal a person but not the user*

SwiftRun – *Able to run at incredible speeds*

Deparo – *Able to disappear for seconds. Longer, depending on the user's power*

Cloudoose – *Clouds appear to create cover for escaping*

Scolifix – *A forbidden spell used to absorb an opponent's life force*

Fluse 'sposure – *A light brightens the area and brings an opponent out of hiding*

Wharsh – *A blast of water shoots out of the user's hand*

Vlornoc – *A spell that gives strength to the user*

Fileepio – *A wisp of fire shoots out of the user's hand to burn something*

Con para fornar recta – *Easy levitating spell*

Gorgo – *An easy lifting spell*

Bargo – *Fires a blast at an enemy*

Succuption – *Vine-like ropes close around an enemy*

Metio Verte – *A melting spell*

Con'tride – *Binds the victim in invisible ropes and tightens slowly*

Felieesous – *A levitating spell with a slight boost of power. It can also shoot an energy attack.*

Meschespa Vintigara – *Give life to plants. As an alternative, it's used as an energy blast.*

Vinlux Disparia – *Capable of making everything appear to be normal (someone who wishes to remain hidden).*

Quespri – *A transport spell only used to on planet Vrec and only used on transporter relics.*

Vin Lux Cumei – *Devastating spell that attacks the insides of an individual if used successfully.*

Bargo Excamei – *Utilizing another spell word, this spell can obliterate anything in its way.*

Mumeius Vecento – *Used to levitate user.*

Quipistorah – *A high level wizarding transport spell.*

ZesCuul Prelor – *A higher level blast beam similar but deadlier to Nozespro Cuulazostras.*

KAKLISTA

Kaklista is the ancient form of magic known to certain wizards, hunters, and huntresses. Kaklista is off-brand magic. A form of Xeiar spells.

Resposha – *A magical beam of light energy.*

Resposheer – *A magical barrier that reflects any physical being.*

Ranchuse – *A spell used to create a secure area, staying hidden. Can use for training purposes.*

Resmend – *A powerful spell used to make anything freeze in time for a few seconds.*

APPENDIX 8

CHARACTER STATS

ShaVenger
Aliases: Joel Rodriguez
Species: Cross-Human
Specialty Item: V-Link *(A VLORs-made, remade by VICE. Used primarily for teleporting.)*
Abilities:

o   Liquid Mimicry

Joel can turn his body all black. In this form, he is able to stretch his limbs to any length. He can also turn his body into a black-purple liquid. This happened when he first became a cross-human. The times to witness the black-purple liquid is when he's doing his trademark skill Liquid Teleportation. His black-purple body spins in a circle and it may or may not resemble a liquefied state.

o   Liquid Teleportation

He is only able to do this when his body is completely turned black. He changes into a liquid, by spiraling himself. He forms a complete circle and then he teleports to another location. This method of transportation is sketchy. He hardly uses ever it.

- o Portal Creation

He can create dark portals similar to the way DiLusion (his mentor) can create portals. He cannot travel long distances utilizing this ability.

- o Hand-to-Hand Combat
- o Exceptional marksman
- o Gymnast

Floral

Aliases: Eraine Delpro've
Species: Cross-Human
Specialty Item: V-Link *(A VICE-made gadget, used primarily for teleporting.)*
Abilities:

- o Chlorokinesis
- o Hand-to-Hand Combat
- o Quick-witted
- o Intelligence *(Capable)*
- o Possesses Leader Traits

Valery 'Veri' Maxill

Date of Birth: January 2nd 2095
Species: Human / Quinoragoras
Abilities:

- o Endurance
- o Expert in Hand-to-Hand Combat
- o Super Strength
- o Resilience

Jayla Price

Species: Xeiar Wizard
Special Ability: Empath

- Empaths are highly sensitive, finely tuned instruments when it comes to emotions. They feel everything, sometimes to an extreme, and are less apt to intellectualize feelings. Intuition is the filter through which they experience the world. Empaths are naturally giving, spiritually attuned, and good listeners. Jayla is learning how to project her mind into others. She can see into the future and past, but only if she's touching something.

Other Abilities:

- o Endurance
- o Moderately trained in Hand-to-Hand Combat *(trained by Valery mid- Book 4)*
- o Super Resilience

Alecxander Jackson

Aliases: Shocker
Species: Shoc'Weillers / Jolt'Tweillers *(Basically Human)*
Abilities:

- o Electrokinesis

He can control, manipulate energies, and generate electricity using the mind.

o   Electrical Absorption

He can absorb anything that holds electricity then he visualizes the electricity coming inside his hand. Important! He cannot let the energies reach the heart!

o   Electri-Ball

A Shoc'Tweillers unique technique. Utilizing precise movements and concentration, a person channels static electricity in their bodies to bring it out as an orb-like shape.

o   Electric Strike

He closes his eyes and visualizes himself standing in an open-wide area. Electricity starts running through his arm. He channels (he must do) and controls it. When he is ready, he can fire it wherever he wants it to go.

o   Electriweaponize

He uses the electrical energy inside of him and uses it to materialize a weapon of choice. A strong opponent can materialize many weapons but not at the same time.

o   Volte-Face

An enemy sends lightning (or similar energy) at him. He breathes out slowly then he positions his hands out in front of him just when the attack is coming at him. He deflects it, but instead of pushing it away he creates an electric orb of energy out of the energy attack. Doing this attack can add three times the power.

o   Transfer

He absorbs electricity then touches something else electronic. He'll be able to visualize the vibrations traveling into the object you're touching.

- o   Expert in Martial Arts
- o   Quick-witted
- o   High Level Intelligence

DiLusion

Aliases: Lilori Daniels *(Human)* and DiLuAH *(Morphenile)*
Species: Morphenile
Specialty Item: Dimension-Travel Device *(Only able to travel to a dark and desolate dimension.)*
Abilities:

- o   Endurance
- o   Moderately skilled in Martial Arts
- o   Super Strength
- o   Resilience
- o   High Level Intelligence
- o   Portal Creation

He can create dark portals.

- o   Liquid Teleportation

He is only able to do this when his body is completely turned black. He changes into a liquid, by spiraling himself. He forms a complete circle and then he teleports to another location. This method of transportation is sketchy. He hardly uses ever it.

      o   Portal Creation

He can create dark portals. He cannot travel long distances utilizing this ability.

Ryan Zada Jones
Date of Birth: November 28th 2094
Aliases: Zadarion / Agent Z / Vex Z / Kewin
Species: Human
Specialty Item: Shibarian Blade
V-Link *(Suit enhances physical body)*
Vex-Armor Emblem *(Suit enhances physical body and human attributes)*
Mysterious Armband *(Located on the upper part of his right arm)*
Abilities:

      o   Endurance *(as Agent Z and Vex Z)*
      o   Expert in Hand-to-Hand Combat
      o   High Level Intelligence *(He hides it.)*
      o   Super Strength *(as Agent Z)*
      o   Super Speed *(as Vex Z)*
      o   Resilience

Mhariah Zari Johnson
Date of Birth: November 28th 2094
Aliases: Zhariah / Agent Rahz / Mira
Species: Human?
Specialty Item: Vactra Daggers
V-Link *(Suit enhances physical body)*
Abilities:

      o   Endurance *(as Agent Rahz)*
      o   Expert in Hand-to-Hand Combat

- o   Moderate Level of Intelligence
- o   Super Strength *(as Agent Rahz)*
- o   Super Speed *(as Agent Rahz utilizing flight boots)*
- o   Resilience

Jack McKoy

Aliases: Agent Caj / Cyprian Keene *(impersonates)* Mr. Colussen *(impersonates)*
Species: Human
Specialty Item: Vactra Cutters
V-Link *(Suit enhances physical body)*
Abilities:

- o   Endurance *(as Agent Caj)*
- o   Expert in Hand-to-Hand Combat
- o   Expert in Nuaiatsu
- o   Moderate Level of Intelligence
- o   Super Strength *(as Agent Caj)*
- o   Super Speed *(Utilizing a Ren tah Chu technique)*
- o   Resilience

Attacks:

- o   **Zhules Gun** – *A technique used to copy an opponent's moveset, speed and power. The more skilled the user, the stronger the move.*
- o   **Water Trailler** – *A move used to run on water in a sprint.*

SAB AI

Date of Creation:
Aliases: Saber LeNosha

Species: Robotic Android
Specialty Item: None
Abilities:

- o   Endurance
- o   Expert in Hand-to-Hand Combat
- o   High Level of Intelligence
- o   Super Strength
- o   Super Speed
- o   Resilience

Attacks:

- o   **Defense Maneuver 12** – *Rocket Launchers shoot out of arms*
- o   **Defense Maneuver 11** – *Extreme Speed Mode - Body becomes fast*
- o   **Defense Maneuver 10** – *Rapid Endurance*
- o   **Defense Maneuver 09** – *Stronghold Guard Mode*
- o   **Defense Maneuver 08** – *Mimicry Mode*
- o   **Defense Maneuver 07** – *Blaster Cannon*
- o   **Defense Maneuver 06** – *Regeneration*
- o   **Defense Maneuver 05** – *Lightning Displacement*
- o   **Defense Maneuver 04** – *Depth Enhancing*
- o   **Defense Maneuver 03** – *Aquatic Enhancers*
- o   **Defense Maneuver 02** – *Heat and Cold Durability Enhancing*
- o   **Defense Maneuver 01** – *Mind Borrowing*
- o   **Defense Maneuver 00** – *Fusion*

Derick Jackson

Aliases: Tundarick
Species: Shoc'Weillers *(Basically Human)*
Abilities:

    o   Electrokinesis

He can control, manipulate energies, and generate electricity using the mind.

    o   Electrical Absorption

He can absorb anything that holds electricity then he visualizes the electricity coming inside his hand. Important! He cannot let the energies reach the heart!

    o   Electri-Ball

A Shoc'Tweillers unique technique. Utilizing precise movements and concentration, a person channels static electricity in their bodies to bring it out as an orb-like shape.

    o   Electric Strike

He closes his eyes and visualizes himself standing in an open-wide area. Electricity starts running through his arm. He channels (he must do) and controls it. When he is ready, he can fire it wherever he wants it to go.

    o   Electriweaponize

He uses the electrical energy inside of him and uses it to materialize a weapon of choice. A strong opponent can materialize many weapons but not at the same time.

- o Volte-Face

An enemy sends lightning (or similar energy) at him. He breathes out slowly then he positions his hands out in front of him just when the attack is coming at him. He deflects it, but instead of pushing it away he creates an electric orb of energy out of the energy attack. Doing this attack can add three times the power.

- o Transfer

He absorbs electricity then touches something else electronic. He'll be able to visualize the vibrations traveling into the object you're touching.

- o Advanced Expert in Ancient Martial Arts
- o Quick-Movements
- o Moderate Level Intelligence

Gunther Jackson

Aliases: Gai Tunh Chi

Species: Shoc'Weillers Guardian *(Basically Human)*

Abilities:

- o Electrokinesis

He can control, manipulate energies, and generate electricity using the mind.

o   Electrical Absorption

He can absorb anything that holds electricity then he visualizes the electricity coming inside his hand. Important! He cannot let the energies reach the heart!

o   Electri-Ball

A Shoc'Tweillers unique technique. Utilizing precise movements and concentration, a person channels static electricity in their bodies to bring it out as an orb-like shape.

o   Electric Strike

He closes his eyes and visualizes himself standing in an open-wide area. Electricity starts running through his arm. He channels (he must do) and controls it. When he is ready, he can fire it wherever he wants it to go.

o   Electriweaponize

He uses the electrical energy inside of him and uses it to materialize a weapon of choice. A strong opponent can materialize many weapons but not at the same time.

o   Volte-Face

An enemy sends lightning (or similar energy) at him. He breathes out slowly then he positions his hands out in front of him just when the attack is coming at him. He deflects it, but instead of pushing it away he creates an electric orb of energy out of the energy attack. Doing this attack can add three times the power.

     o   Transfer

He absorbs electricity then touches something else electronic. He'll be able to visualize the vibrations traveling into the object you're touching.

     o   Deat'Low *Jolt'Tweillers Technique*

This move can immobilize a person and it infects them with a horrendous illness that will eventually be their cause of death. The technique is very difficult to master.

     o   Advanced Expert in Ancient Martial Arts
     o   Advanced Quick-Movements
     o   Advanced Level Intelligence
     o   Advanced Knowledge of the Earth and its History *Past down from Guardian to Guardian telepathically. Bestowed to all future Guardians at birth and fully activates in the mind once they take over as Guardian.*

A SNEAK PEEK…

VLORs & VICE: The ZERO Series!

A teenage Richard Maxill is taken over by the revived Quinorgoras King. He chuckles as he watches from the newly built tower on planet Devina while the Devion race are hard at work. Malvin, Dextorey, Tora, and Tora's weak little assistant, the King's last surviving General's, has taken refuse on the planet five years after the Damonarian v. Quinoragoras War. These four had no part in the war.

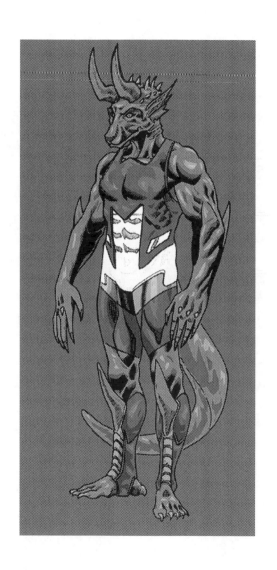

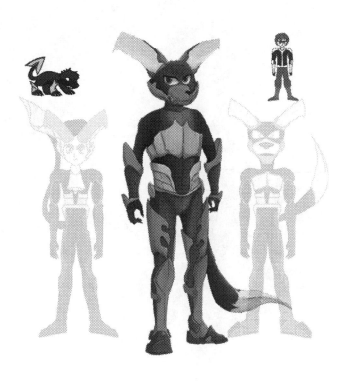

ASARIOS
X
MALEENA

Asarios
XEIAR Wizard

Maleena
XEIAR Wizard

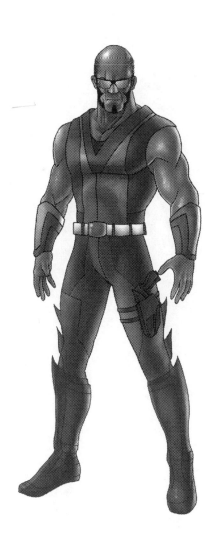

Printed in the United States
By Bookmasters